I0451379

Ten Days in Heaven

SAMANTHA MICHAELS

Copyright © 2023 by Samantha Myers

All rights reserved.

No part of this book may be reproduced in any form or by any electronic or mechanical means, including information storage and retrieval systems, without written permission from the author, except for the use of brief quotations in a book review.

❀ Created with Vellum

First and foremost, I need to thank my husband and my dog for being my biggest supporters!
To my amazing author besties JJ Grice and LaLa Montgomery, I love you both to the moon and back!
Thank you to my amazing PA Ayana and the team at Carxander Publishing!
Thank you to Alyssa for the amazing job proofreading!
And finally, thank you to the readers for taking a chance on me!

Prologue

RILEY

* * *

I still can't believe he did this to me. I'm Riley Cavanaugh, a pathetic loser who's spending another lonely Friday night in my pajamas. I put the TV on and tune into a marathon of my favorite comfort show, Friends. I should have been spending tonight making final preparations for my trip to Hawaii. I really need my best friend, but I was too embarrassed to tell her what happened. I kept my time off so I didn't have to explain anything. Plus, it gives me a chance to sit and wallow.

Nights like these remind me of my childhood. I was shy and had very few friends, so I spent most of my time reading. I always imagined myself being in the books I was reading, which helped with my loneliness. Now that I'm older, I've taken up writing as a form of therapy. I get up and grab my laptop.

I open a blank document and sit and stare at it for a few minutes. Suddenly, Ace's handsome face pops into my head. That's all the inspiration I need and I start typing. Fictional Riley runs into fictional Ace. After she tells him what happened with her trip, he comes to the rescue and gives her ten days she'll never forget.

It takes me a few days to finish the story. After I type 'the end,' I print a copy and read it. I must say, I'm pleased with how it turned out. I know two things for sure. First, anyone who reads it is going to need a cold shower. Second, one of those people can never be Ace!

CHAPTER 1
Riley

* * *

"Earth to Riley. Come in, Riley."

I look up and see my best friend Maddie standing in front of me, I can't help but wonder how long she's been trying to get my attention.

"Sorry. My brain already thinks it's in Hawaii."

"Bitch! If you weren't my bestie, I'd hate you."

"But you are, so you have to love me!"

"Can I wait until you're back home?"

"Deal."

"Besides, you'll be making it up to me."

"How?"

"Don't pretend you forgot. Our 30th high school reunion."

"Fine, if you insist." I sigh.

"Damn right I do. I wonder if you-know-who's coming?"

"Don't know, don't care."

"Come on, he was your best friend, after me, of course."

"Then he left and forgot all about me."

"Fame will do that to a guy, especially playing lead guitar for one of the top metal bands." She says.

"Big damn deal. Besides, I have Brad."

"Yawn city. Sorry for saying that, but he's no Ace."

"You're right about that. He would never leave me like that."

"I bet Ace is better in bed."

"Brad is just fine in that area."

"Just fine? Oh, that sounds exciting. Guess you keep plenty of batteries around."

"Madison Jane Elliott!" I exclaim.

"Don't pretend you don't. You're not the innocent angel everyone here thinks you are."

"This from the president of the Man of the Month Club."

"I'm not only the president, I'm also a member."

"That's the Hair Club, dingbat!"

Maddie stuck her tongue out at me then headed back to her desk. My mind wanders to thoughts of him. Not the him I should be thinking of, but rather the sexy rock star that used to be my friend. I wish I'd had the guts to tell him how I felt. Too late now. Plus, I have Brad. But, I can't help but wonder what my life would be like if I had told him.

I shake my head and return my attention back to the boring spreadsheet I've been staring at. Most of the time, I enjoy my job. I like researching and resolving problems. Sometimes, though, my boss needs me to perform more tedious tasks, like this report I'm working on. Never have I been happier to see 3:30 than I am today. I'm just finishing shutting down my computer when Maddie stops at my desk.

"Get a move on it, woman. Paradise awaits."

"I have to get home and pack my batteries."

"Ha, ha. Seriously, though, are you all packed?"

"I packed most of my stuff last night. Just need to do my toiletries." I smile.

"That's my predictable friend."

"I am NOT predictable!"

"Yes, you are, but that's why I love you. You keep me grounded."

"Thanks."

When we get down to the parking lot, Maddie gives me a hug. I spend my whole ride home thinking about what she said. Good old boring Riley. Everyone can count on Riley. Just once, I want to be "shocks the shit out of everyone" Riley. But, I can't complain. Tomorrow, I'll be relaxing on a beach in Hawaii. AC/DC's Back in Black takes me out of my reverie. I look at my phone and see Brad's face.

"Hey. Brad. I was just finishing up packing."

"Yeah, well, you can unpack."

"Excuse me?"

"Darcy's coming with me?" He states.

"Again, excuse me? I'm your girlfriend."

"You were my girlfriend."

"Excuse me? You're dumping me?"

"Yeah, you're boring as fuck. I'd much rather be with Darcy. Have a nice life."

Before I can respond, Brad disconnects the call.

"Asshole! Who the fuck does he think he is?"

I trudge out to the couch, sit down, and grab my Ace London pillow. I clutch it to my chest. Despite him leaving me and our friendship behind, I still support him, regularly shopping in his online merch shop. Holding the pillow tight, I start picturing what my life would be like if he was still in it. He never knew it, but I had a crush on him. I never even told Maddie about that, as she would have just teased me.

I see us in a house by a beach in California. The walls are plastered with platinum and gold records, along with tons of pictures. We have an indoor hot tub, game room and a music room in addition to all the standard rooms. Of course, since he's made it big, I don't have to have a 9-5. Instead, I get to focus on my writing. I'm obsessed with writing and reading smut. I once shared that with Brad and he got offended. I would love to find a man to read dirty stuff to me in bed.

An hour into my self-pity party, I hear my stomach rumble. I head down to Angelo's, my favorite pizza place, might as well drown my misery in some pizza and beer. I jump in my sexy red 1965 convertible Mustang. I pull into the parking lot, and stare at the building for a couple of minutes before I go in. I've been coming here since high school and nothing has changed.

I'm relieved when I see my favorite table is open. I like sitting in the back corner, especially when I'm here alone. I feel a sense of comfort when I look around. The same red and white checkered tablecloths cover each table. The walls are filled with pictures of Angelo and his family. The counter at the front of the restaurant is flanked on each side by a bakery case filled with delicious desserts. Angelo's wife Maria bakes everything from scratch. I plan on putting a dent in one of the chocolate cakes before I leave. Maria stopped by my table to take my order.

"What's troubling you?" She asks me in her thick Italian accent.

"Brad dumped me."

"He's a fool. I can put a curse on him."

I laugh through my tears. "That won't be necessary, but thank you."

"What can I get for you?"

"A man. Seriously, I would like a pizza with pepperoni and extra cheese."

"Anything to drink, honey?"

"A pitcher of beer."

"I can bring you all but the man." She smiles.

A few minutes later, Angelo brings me my beer and two glasses.

"I only need one glass."

He puts both glasses on the table, smiles, and walks away without saying a word. Leave it to Angelo to make it look like I'm not alone. He's the sweetest man. A fresh round of tears fills my green eyes and I look down at my lap, hoping nobody sees me.

"Your pizza, sweetie," Maria says warmly.

"Thank you."

I lower my head back down, still trying to fight the tears that sting my eyes. I hear the door open, looking up to see and my jaw drops. It can't be. I must be hallucinating, but I'm not. Standing in front of the restaurant, in all his glory, stands Angus 'Ace' London. I haven't seen him in person since the summer after we graduated from high school. Pictures haven't done this man justice.

He's six feet, four inches of chiseled muscles. My fingers ache to get tangled in his golden brown hair, hanging just below his broad shoulders. His day-old beard makes his face even more handsome. And hot damn, the dimples that appear when he smiles are impossible to resist. I feel a heat spread between my legs. I see him speak to Angelo, who leads him to a table at the other side of the restaurant. I have no idea if he saw me.

CHAPTER 2

Ace

* * *

"**A**ce Fuckin' London!" Mark yells way too loudly.

He gives me a big "bro" hug. Mark's been my best friend since kindergarten. I can't think of anyone who I'd want to see first. Well, maybe one other person. I wonder what she's up to tonight. I sit down across from Mark. He has a pitcher of beer and two glasses waiting for me. He pours us each a beer.

"To getting old," he jokes as we clink glasses.

I take a sip of beer then ask, "What've you been up to?"

"Jenny and I have been working on the house. Now that we're empty-nesters, we have a couple of spare rooms."

"What are you planning to do with them?"

"One's going to be a home gym. We're still not sure about the other."

"What about a hot tub?"

"I may have to run that by Jenny. How lame are we? Sitting here talking home improvements."

"Not lame at all. I would trade places with you in a second." I say.

"You're fuckin' crazy. Look at the life you've had. Touring, parties, women."

"Yeah, it was fun. But, there's always been something missing."

"Something or someone?"

"Shut it."

"Hit a nerve, did I?" Mark teases me.

"I fucked up and I know it. It's only ever been her. Now, it's too late."

"Don't be so sure."

"Huh? She's with someone."

"Then, why's she sitting at her favorite table alone?"

I stand up and turn where Mark's pointing. I find myself just staring at her. I always thought she was cute in high school. Time has been kind to her and she's moved way beyond cute. This woman is stunning. Her chestnut colored hair begs for my fingers. I see tears staining her cheek and I feel an anger rise up in my gut. Who the fuck made this woman cry? He better hope I never get my hands on him. She suddenly looks up and her mouth drops. Even with her red puffy eyes, she's still by far the most beautiful woman I've ever seen. I get up and go take a seat across from her.

"Riley Cavanaugh as I live and breathe. Beautiful as ever, love."

"Yeah, right. I must look wonderful."

"To me you do. Time's been kind to you. What have you been up to since high school?"

"I graduated from Penn State with a bachelor's degree in Information Technology. After graduation, I got a job at a top healthcare company, who paid for my Master's degree. I've worked there since, and am now a senior technician."

"I always knew you were smart."

"Thanks. I know what you've been up to, but I would love to hear some stories."

"You'd be disappointed. I wasn't keen on the rockstar life. I loved the music and playing in front of crowds. What I didn't like was the way my bandmates treated women like objects."

"Really? I thought that's why guys got into music."

"That's how we're all portrayed, but not all of us. I always wanted a relationship."

"Me too. And until tonight, I was in one."

"So, that's what's wrong. Who did this to you?"

"Please, my stupid issues are not your problem."

"Like hell. I want to know who the fuck hurt you." I say angrily.

She doesn't respond and I'm afraid I came on too strong.

"Sorry, doll. I just hate that someone upset you. Tell me what happened."

"I guess, but first, would you like a beer and some pizza?"

"I'd love some."

I pour two glasses and give her one. Our hands touch when she takes the glass and I feel electricity course through my body. What the fuck? I can't possibly still have a thing for this woman, can I? I wanted desperately to ask her out in high school, but I was afraid what it might do to our friendship. I've been following her on social media and she's been in relationships, so I thought I missed my shot. Maybe our reunion is exactly what was meant to bring us together.

She sighs and begins, "I was seeing this guy Brad. He was a nice guy, but kinda boring."

"In what way?"

"Well, you know I always had a thing for reading smut? Well, I tried reading him some once and he told me was offended. I thought it would turn him on."

"Uhhh...what the fuck? I'd be hard in two seconds flat."

I stifle a laugh as her cheeks turn bright red. Fuck, I feel my dick starting to stir. What the hell is this woman doing to me?

"Well, anyway, he was a decent boyfriend, or so I thought. We were supposed to leave for a ten day vacation tomorrow morning."

"Supposed to?"

"He called me tonight to tell me he was taking his stupid bitch of an assistant instead. Fucker."

"Where does he live?" I growl.

"Why?"

"I'm gonna go kick the shit out of him."

"That's not necessary, but I appreciate the sentiment."

"Fine. So, I know I haven't kept in touch like I should've. Tell me what else has been going on."

"Nothing exciting. My job's okay, and I work with Maddie but she has the habit of telling me that I'm predictable. And sadly, she's not wrong."

"So, stop being predictable."

"Easy for you to say. I need to keep a routine. I need to go to my job every day and pay my bills every month. We can't all be badass rock stars who forget their friends." She smiles sadly.

"Ouch, but I do deserve that. I really am sorry, doll."

"Whatever. It's ancient history. Let's just enjoy the rest of this pizza and beer."

I watch more tears form in her eyes and my rage returns. All I can think about is kicking Brad's ass. Well, that and how much I want this woman in my bed. I picture her lying there naked, just waiting for me to give her the pleasure she deserves. How the fuck could anyone think another woman was better than her? I fucked up when I left her. I can't fuck up again.

We enjoy the rest of our meal, while I tell her some of the more horrific stories of being a rock star. Nothing was worse than having women sneak into my hotel room or the tour bus. Most of the other musicians I met over the years loved that but not me. I've always been a relationship guy. Sure, I had my fair share of one night stands, but I only ever wanted her. The beautiful Riley Cavanaugh.

"So, tell me. What do you and Maddie do for fun?" I ask.

"We love hitting the local rock club. Lots of great music plus amazing men to pick from. And it's about to get even better."

"How so?"

"New ownership. Sadly, the previous owner passed away. He left the club to his friend, and she's expanding it to also include a bookstore. That's perfect for me. Alcohol and books are a winning combination."

"Doug passed away? Damn, what happened?"

"You knew him?" She asks.

"Yeah, I played here when his dad was still the owner, and we became friends. Until I left."

"Sounds familiar. He was out for a walk with his wife. They were crossing the road when someone ran a red light. Neither survived."

"That's awful. I'm so sorry to hear. Know anything about the new owner?"

"I know her name's Lexi. She seems cool and she has a rock star for a boyfriend. Ever heard of Damien St. James?"

"Yeah. He's fuckin' amazing. I'd love to meet him."

"I'm friends with the bartender, so might be able to score a meeting."

"Cool. But now back to you, doll. What else have you been up to?"

"Not much besides my job. Even less now that Brad sent me packing. Tomorrow, I would have been in Hawaii for the first time ever. Now I have to spend the next ten days hiding. I don't want anyone to know what he did to me."

Without warning, an idea pops into my head. But, will she go for it? If I play it right, I can meet her needs, and satisfy my anaconda at the same time. I try to imagine what it feels like inside her. I need to find out, but only if she accepts my proposition.

"I have an idea, love."

"Oh, is that so? Judging by the look on your face, I'm intrigued."

"You mentioned everyone thinking you're predictable and that you need to hide. I can help with both."

"How so?"

"Spend those ten days with me. Imagine the fun we could have. And don't tell me that doesn't interest you."

"I can't."

"Give me one good reason." I demand.

"What would people say?"

"Who gives a shit. What do you want to do?"

"Say goodbye to Miss Practicality!"

"Doll, you're in for one hell of a good time!"

"I better be!"

"I'll send a car for you in the morning."

"Can't wait."

We talk a little while longer until Angelo brings the check. It's getting near closing time so I grab the check.

"What are you doing?" she asks.

"Treating you to dinner, love."

"That's not necessary."

"I want to."

"Thanks."

I walk her to her car. Before she gets in, I grab her hand and kiss the back of it.

"I'll see you in the morning."

Before she can answer, I turn and walk away. I watch her get in her car and head home. I do the same, as I have a lot of plans to make!

CHAPTER 3
Riley

* * *

I 'm sitting on my porch, questioning if last night actually happened or if I was dreaming. As if it manifested itself to answer my question, a white limo pulls into my driveway. The driver gets out and approaches my porch.

"Good morning, ma'am. My name is Bruce. Mr. London sent me to pick you up. May I load your luggage?"

"Yes, please."

"Very well."

I watch Bruce load my bags into the trunk. He opens the back door for me. After I climb in, he closes it and gets into the driver seat. He pulls out of my driveway and heads toward what I presume is Ace's home. I'm a bundle of nerves and excitement. It's been too long since I've had sex. Brad had stopped touching me. I thought he was just stressed at work, not that he was fucking that bitch.

To hell with him. I'm going to spend ten days with a hot, sexy rockstar. Someone I always had a crush on. And now I'm going to stay at his house. But do I have the guts to let him see me naked? No way in hell. I'm sure he saw the hottest women on earth during his travels. No way I could compare to any of them. What the hell was I thinking, agreeing to this? I'm about to tell Bruce to take me back home when he pulls into the driveway of the most beautiful home I've ever laid eyes on.

The outside is all freshly painted red brick with black shutters on all the windows. From the outside, it appears the house has three floors. I can't wait to see what's behind the beautiful cedar colored double doors. Each door is carved with a beautiful guitar and features a small stained glass window on top. Bruce opens my door and helps me exit the limo. He grabs my bags out of the trunk. We walk together to the front door, where he rings the bell. My knees go weak when the door opens.

Ace is standing there in tight black leather pants and a black button-down shirt. I love the fact that musicians don't know how to work buttons. I stand there gawking at the sexiest chest I've ever seen. His upper chest is covered with dark hair, just enough to make my panties melt. My eyes follow the trail of hair starting under his navel. I start to picture where that leads and my heart races. And don't get me started on those pants... Holy hell, they leave little to the imagination. Is he smuggling an eggplant in there?

"Thank you, Bruce, for safely delivering this beauty." Ace says.

He flashes that million dollar smile and his dimples appear. I go weak in the knees. He grabs my arm and keeps me from going down. I turn fifteen shades of red when I see Ace and Bruce stifling a laugh. I pretend to be pissed, but secretly, my skin is on fire where he's touching me.

"Is there anything else you need, sir?" Bruce asks.

"No, thank you."

Bruce gets back in his limo and heads out of Ace's horseshoe driveway. Ace picks up my suitcase.

"Shall we go inside, doll?"

"Yes, please."

I follow Ace into the foyer and my jaw drops. The house is stunning. The floor is hardwood with small carpet at the doorway. I look at Ace, who's standing there with a smile on his handsome face.

"Would you like a tour?" he asks.

"Ummm, okay."

What the hell is wrong with me? I'm an intelligent, educated woman and I can barely remember how to speak. To be fair, Ace is the hottest guy on this entire planet. Hell, he might even be the hottest guy in the universe. He takes me into his kitchen, and I'm jealous. I love to cook and would give anything to have that much space. Not to mention what I imagine him doing to me on one of those marble counters. The rest of the first floor has a half-bath, an entertainment room, and an indoor hot tub.

He walks me to the far wall, where I see an elevator. A fucking elevator in his damn house. Holy shit, I could get used to this. He presses the button and we go inside. Again, my mind goes in the gutter. We get to the second floor. I see three doors along the hallway along with sliding glass doors that open to a large balcony. Two of the hallway doors are bedrooms and one is a bathroom. The bathroom includes a walk-in shower and a separate tub for two. Oh, the fun to be had here.

Back inside the elevator, we reach the top floor. He shows me one more bedroom. There's a second door, but we don't go inside. In fact, he doesn't even acknowledge that door. I wonder what's inside. He walks me back to the elevator so we can return to the living room.

Ace walks over to the stereo and puts on some romantic music. He takes me into his arms and I notice how great he smells. Without a word he gently lifts my chin and gives me the sweetest, most passionate kiss I've ever felt. We dance and kiss for several more songs and I'm starting to feel better. I can't believe I'm in Ace's living room, his lips on mine as his tongue dances in my mouth. His words snap me back to reality,

"You're an amazing kisser. I can only imagine what else you're amazing at. I wanna take you to bed and find out." Ace says.

"You could have any woman you want. You don't need someone horrible enough that she was cheated on." I responded.

"You're only partially right, baby. It's true that I've never had a problem finding a woman. But those women were never anything more than a fuck. There's only one woman I've always loved, and that's you. Let me prove it to you."

"Don't waste your time. Brad told me I'm boring. Actually, boring as fuck is what he said."

"Why would he say that?"

"I'm guessing he found me boring in the sack, since he cheated. In all fairness to me, he only had one move and never once gave me an orgasm."

"A beautiful doll like you?"

"Yeah, right."

"By the time this stay-cation ends, I'm going to prove to you that you're stunning. Come with me."

Words escape me, and all I can do is nod yes. Ace holds out his hand, which I take. He leads me to the elevator. The minute we're inside, his hands are all over me. My entire body's on fire and my panties are soaked. He scoops me up in his arms, and when the doors open, he carries me to his bedroom. He puts me down and just stands there, staring at me.

After a few minutes, he grabs me and pulls me in tight, crushing his lips to mine. I feel his tongue eagerly exploring my mouth and I can barely stand. If he wasn't holding me, I'd have hit the floor.

"Babe, I need to ask you something," Ace says.

"Sure."

"Are you comfortable with me telling you what to do?"

"You mean...in here?" I say shyly.

"Yeah, sweetie."

"Ummm...nobody's ever done that. But, okay."

"I promise I won't be mean." he says, reassuring me.

"Okay."

"Good. Now, get that hot little ass on my bed."

His command excites me, and I climb onto the bed. I'm not normally someone who likes being ordered around, but something about him doing it is exciting. Or, maybe it's where he's doing it that's turning me on.

"Eyes on me, woman." he says sternly.

I watch as he slowly strips for me. I've seen him in only swim trunks before, but never completely naked. When he slides his boxers down and kicks them off, my eyes go wide. Holy shit. I could tell it was big when I saw the bulge in his pants, but damn. I suddenly start to panic. What if I can't handle him? I can't take another man making me feel bad about myself. I start to get up, but his sharp command stops me.

"Don't you dare get off that bed."

I try to catch my breath, but I can't. I put my hand over my chest, and I see his face soften.

"Riley, are you okay?"

I nod, unable to form words. He lies down next to me and caresses my cheek.

"Tell me what's wrong," he says softly.

"I'm scared."

"Of what?"

"You," I whisper.

"But, you said you were okay with me ordering you around."

"Not that. I'm afraid of your dick."

"Okay, doll, you need to explain. I'm missing something."

"You're so...ummm...massive. What if I can't handle you?"

He starts laughing uncontrollably, but he stops when he sees that I'm not laughing with him.

"I'm sorry, doll, I shouldn't have laughed at you. I promise I'll go slow."

I suddenly realize how stupid and inexperienced I sounded and my face turns bright red.

"Babe, don't be embarrassed. Just lie back, relax, and let me work my magic."

He kisses me softly, as his hands slide under my shirt. His hands feel so good on my skin. I'm thankful I chose a front-closure bra today when I feel him open it with ease. His hands massage my boobs and a moan escapes my lips. He slides my shirt off of me, and tosses it along with my bra onto the floor.

"Baby, so beautiful." he murmurs into my ear.

He covers one of my boobs with his mouth, flicking at my hard nipple with his tongue, while teasing the other with his hand. He runs his tongue down to my stomach, setting my skin on fire. He's so close to where I want him most. My breathing shallows as I anticipate feeling his tongue between my thighs.

"Tell me what you want, doll." Ace says.

I'm too embarrassed, so I keep quiet.

"I guess you don't want anything then. If you can't tell me, I can't pleasure you."

I take a deep breath.

"I want to feel your tongue."

"Where?"

"You know where."

"Tell me, woman. I wanna hear those filthy words coming out of that pretty mouth."

"I want your tongue on my pussy. Please, Ace," I beg.

"Mmmm, good girl."

He rewards me by swiping his tongue between my folds. He slowly drags it over my clit. Damn, it feels so good. I feel my inhibitions slipping away.

"Oh fuck, Ace, suck my clit hard, baby."

What the hell did I just say? Fuck it. He told me he wanted to hear those words. The smile that appears on his face lets me know he likes what he just heard. He responds by doing exactly what I told him to. I quickly explode and my entire body quivers. He keeps sucking on me as wave after wave of glorious pleasure washes over me. He slides up my body, but doesn't enter me. He opens his mouth to say something, but I beat him to it.

"Please, Ace, I need your cock inside me. NOW!"

"Damn, woman, I want you so fucking much."

I feel him enter. He goes slow, allowing me time to adjust to his size. And damn, does it feel good. His dick touches parts of me that none have before. I'm moaning louder than I've ever done, unable to control myself. I've never felt anything like this. Turns out, it's Brad and not me who's the boring one!

"Mmm, Angus, so good."

"Doll, you feel like heaven."

I feel him continue his slow thrusting and I completely come undone again. I scream out a string of obscenities at the top of my lungs as my body bucks off the bed. He must like what he hears as I feel him empty himself inside me. He emits a long, low growl and lies down next to me, pulling me into his muscular arms.

"It feels so right lying in your arms, Ace."

"Did you realize you called me Angus while we were fucking?"

"I did?"

"Yeah. And it was hot."

"What we just did was hot."

"You handled me like a goddess."

Before I can respond, my stomach growls. I'm mortified, especially when I hear Ace laughing.

"I guess you worked up a bit of an appetite, doll. How about we head downstairs and have some lunch?"

"Sounds good."

We get downstairs and I'm in awe at the appliances he has around his huge kitchen. I zero in on one of my favorites.

"How about quesadillas?" I ask.

"I've never made them. I bought the maker but never tried it."

"You're looking at an expert. They're quick and easy, so I make them quite often for myself. Mind if I snoop in your fridge?"

"Snoop away, my sexy doll."

I grab some shredded cheese and bacon. I ask Ace for a skillet so I can cook the bacon then put the quesadilla together. After it's ready, I cut it up and top it with some salsa.

"Damn, a woman who can cook in the kitchen and the bedroom! Might just have to keep you."

"Dickhead!"

"Damn right."

We finish eating and Ace helps me clean up. Such a difference from Brad, who let me do everything.

"So, doll, this is your vacation. What would you like to do next?"

"I would love a soak in your hot tub. Let's get naked again."

"What have you done with Miss Innocent Riley?"

"You've awakened Riley 2.0."

"Finally!" He cheers.

"Could not agree more. I actually feel alive for the first time in quite a while."

We get in the elevator and head to the second floor. Once we're in his bathroom, he pulls me in close. He crushes his lips to mine and I can feel his erection straining against his pants. Fuck, I wanna taste him. I pull away from him and get on my knees in front of him. I unfasten his pants and slide them down along with his underwear, freeing the beast.

I open wide and take his dick into my mouth. I take him all the way down my throat, surprised that I'm not gagging.

"Fuck, baby, nobody's ever been able to handle me like you."

I suck hard and fast until he fills my mouth. I look up at him and swallow every last delicious drop. All he can do is growl. He removes the rest of his clothing and opens the hot tub while I strip. I can see the hunger in his eyes when he looks at me, and I'm instantly wet. I picture sitting in his lap and riding him. That would make a huge mess, but I fully intend to ride that man in bed later.

We end up soaking in the hot tub until near-dinner time. We dry off and head down to the kitchen. This time he cooks for me. I'm impressed as hell when he places a plate of homemade chicken Parmesan in front of me. He pours two glasses of wine. We sit at his dining room table, eating, drinking, and laughing.

"How about we head to the living room?" Ace asks after we finish cleaning up.

"Okay."

He snakes his arm around my waist and walks me over to his huge sofa. He pats the cushion next to him, but I pick a different seat. I straddle him and his jaw drops. He puts his arms around me, but before he can say a word, I plant a kiss on his sexy mouth. I run my tongue along his lips and he opens for me, so I jam my tongue into his mouth. I break the kiss.

"I want you out of those pants now," I demand.

He stands and I can see he's ready for me. He removes his clothes and damn, I love seeing him naked. After he sits back down, I give him a naughty striptease. When I'm done, I sit back on his lap, this time, taking his dick inside me. I hold his broad shoulders as I slide up and down on him. I love being in control like this. I position myself for maximum friction. Each time I slide up his dick, my clit rubs against his rock hard erection. He moves his hands to my ass, squeezing as we fuck.

"Oh, fuck, doll. I can't control myself for another second."

I feel him empty inside me and that sends me over the edge. My body convulses as I finish. I collapse against his chest.

"Have you always secretly been like this?" Ace asks me breathlessly.

"I have, but Brad wanted no part of it. I once tried to read to him from the naughty book I was reading, and he wouldn't let me."

"What the fuck? That would turn me the hell on. I hope you brought one with you."

"I have a few tucked in my suitcase."

A wicked grin spreads across his face and I know I'm in for one hell of a staycation. After the day we had, we're both completely spent, so we ride the elevator to the second floor. We didn't even bother getting dressed, and even though the elevator's in his house, it still felt naughty. We climb into his bed. He pulls the cover up and pulls me in close. That's the last thing I remember until morning.

CHAPTER 4

Ace

* * *

The sunlight pouring in my windows awakens me. I reach over and make sure yesterday wasn't a dream. I feel the soft, silky skin of my baby and I can't help but smile. I still can't believe Riley Cavanaugh is naked in my bed. I run my fingers lightly down her back and she stirs. I watch her turn and face me, a sleepy smile on her face.

"Good morning, beautiful." I whisper.

"Mmmm, good morning, sexy." she responds.

"Care to join me for a shower before we have breakfast?"

"Oh, yes. I'd love to."

I watch her get out of bed and grab her toiletry bag. Damn that woman is hot. We walk down to the bathroom and into the shower stall. I turn the water on and pull her in tight. The hot water feels good, but not as good as having her in my arms. I grab her shower gel and squeeze some into my hand, and wash her. I hear her moan softly as my hands explore her skin. I spend some extra time on that hot ass before I rinse her off. I'm aching to run my fingers through her hair, so I grab her shampoo. I inhale the scent of coconut filling my nose.

I would never admit this to the guys, but there's nothing I love more than the scent of women's hair and body care products, especially when that scent lingers on their delicious bodies. I run the shampoo through her hair and massage her scalp. I hear her moan, and my dick stirs. Everything about this woman excites me.

She looks down and smiles. "I guess you really like my hair."

"Baby, I like everything about you."

"Why? I'm boring."

"Doll, you are about as far from boring as anyone I've ever known."

"You're sweet. Now, it's my turn."

I watch her grab my bottle of Bulgari and squeeze some into her hand. She rubs them together and rubs the lather over my body. I notice she spends a bit longer on my dick than anywhere else. I lose the battle, and I'm hard. Fuck, this woman is so damn hot. She washes my hair then rinses me off. I pull her into an embrace and kiss her hard. The feeling of being this close to her with the hot water streaming down our bodies is too much to take. All I think about is being inside her. But, I talk myself down as I have special plans for later.

We get out, get dried off, and get dressed. We head downstairs and I treat her to my famous French toast. After we finish breakfast, we go out to the backyard.

"Babe, I have an idea that I want to run by you."

"Okay, shoot."

"I thought a camping trip would be fun."

"But, I thought the plan was for me to hide out here so nobody knows what happened."

"It is, which is why the camping trip will be right here in my backyard."

"Really?"

"Yeah, I have a tent and sleeping bags in the garage. We can cook out on the grill. Plus I have a fire pit so we can make s'mores. And hey, if we're so inclined, we could have some special fun in the tent." I wink.

"Mmmm...special fun, huh? I have a feeling I'm going to enjoy that."

"So, sound good?"

"Yes it does."

"Cool. For now, how about a dip in the pool?"

"I'd love to. I just need to grab my suit."

"Nah, you don't need it."

"What?"

"Come skinny dipping with me, woman!"

"I can't do that!"

"Why not? I have a privacy fence. Nobody will see us."

"But, I'm not attractive enough." She whispers.

"Doll, you're stunning, I couldn't take my eyes off of you the whole time we were fucking yesterday."

"Still, though..."

"Come on, baby. You said you wanted to be more unpredictable. Get that ass naked and jump in that pool."

"What the hell! Let's go."

I watch Riley run out to the backyard and start stripping. I run out after her just as she jumps in, laughing and splashing around. I love seeing this playful side of her. At that moment, I realize I'm completely in love with this woman, and I always have been. I jump in and swim over to her. I try to grab her but as soon as I get close, she splashes me and swims away. She's in trouble now!

"I'm gonna get you, doll."

"We'll see about that."

She swims away again, but this time I catch her and pull her in close. She tries to pull away but I won't let go. I start tickling her as she laughs hysterically. I've always loved that sound, especially when she does that cute snort. We swim for another hour, then I climb out and grab a couple of towels. I watch Riley climb out of the pool and I'm awestruck by her beauty. I wrap her in a towel, pull her in close, and lay a kiss on her.

"Mmm, I have a feeling I know what's going to happen in that tent tonight." she teases.

"Just you wait, woman."

We get dressed and head to the garage so I can get things set up for later. After we get the tent setup, we head back inside and sit down on the couch, still in our towels. I want this woman so damn bad, I'm not sure I can wait until tonight. And her sitting there in just a towel gives me easy access. I'm craving a taste of that sweet spot between those sexy legs. I stand up, move in front of her, and drop to my knees. I open the towel and admire her sexy curves.

"Spread those beautiful legs, baby. I need to taste you."

She opens her legs for me, and my eyes immediately travel to that sweet pussy.

"I can't believe I'm saying this but I'm turned on by you staring at me like that."

"Is that so, doll? I could sit and look at you all day, but right now, all I want is to take you to heaven with my tongue."

"Yes, please, baby."

I place a hand on each of her shapely thighs and open her legs even wider. I run my tongue up and down her pussy, and fuck, she tastes so damn good. I continue my assault on her until I feel her body quake. I stop and stand up.

"Okay, doll, get on your knees on the couch, facing the back and spread those legs again."

She does as she's told, and after admiring her ass for a few minutes, I lower myself onto the couch and put my head between her thighs. Time to turn this up a notch. I intend to bring out the dirty lioness that lives inside this goddess.

"I wanna watch you get yourself off. Get those hips moving."

I keep my tongue out as she drags that hot pussy back and forth. I watch her tits bouncing as she fucks my tongue and I can barely control myself. I stop her movement and wrap my lips around her swollen clit, sucking hard until she comes hard. I need my dick inside her now.

"Baby, I want you in my lap but with your back against my chest."

"Mmm, Ace." she murmurs as she lowers herself onto my lap, taking my dick deep inside. She slides up and down my dick and shit, it feels incredible. I tease her already-sensitive clit with my fingers as she leans back against my chest. I love feeling every part of this woman against me. She quickly sends me over the edge and I empty inside her. She doesn't move off my lap, so I wrap my arms around her, running my hands up and down her body.

"Oh, baby, you truly were made for me. Your body fits mine perfectly, and I can't get enough of you."

I stop short of telling her I love her. I'm not quite ready to say those words yet. But I definitely do. Ten days with this woman is not nearly enough. What if she doesn't feel the same way? I need to find a way to convince her that we belong together. I don't want to be with any other woman, ever.

"Angus, that was incredible. I was satisfied with my sex life before you, but I realize now how much I was missing."

"There's so much more I can show you, baby."

"Oh god, yes please. Teach me everything."

"Damn," is all I can muster. "For now, I think we need to grab a shower. When we're done, are you ready to start our camping adventure."

"I can't wait. I love...camping."

Holy shit, she almost said it. The thing I most want to hear and the thing I most want to say. I let it go for now, but I will make sure she hears it before these ten days have passed. After a quick shower, we get in our pajamas and head to the kitchen to grab what we need. She helps me carry everything out while I light the fire pit. We cook hot dogs over the fire pit. After we finish eating, I put some music on, and ask her to dance.

I don't take my eyes off of her beautiful face as we sway together to the music. The warm grass feels good on my bare feet. Suddenly, it hits me that I'm standing in my backyard in pajamas with my best friend and I can't stop myself from laughing.

"What's so funny?" she asks.

"I was just thinking about this whole scenario. The two of us dancing in my backyard in pajamas with a tent set up just reminds me of our youth. All those backyard campouts we had. One thing about having your parents and my parents always going to parties for their job gave us the chance to do anything we wanted. If only they could see us now."

"No thank you. I do just fine without them."

"I hear that. I'm sorry I brought them up."

"It's all good. All I care about is being here right now."

She looks up at the sky and a smile appears on her pretty face.

"Remember laying in the grass looking at the stars?" she asks.

"I sure do. Wanna do that?"

"Yeah."

We lay down next to each other, gazing up at the night sky. The moon is full tonight and looks beautiful. It's beauty, though, pales in comparison to my Riley. I grab her hand and she intertwines her fingers with mine.

"I would always think about what the future held for me when we did this." I say.

"And what did you see?"

"Pretty much the life I ended up with. I always knew I wanted to play music. I used to watch shows like MTV's Cribs, and I was determined I would have that lifestyle someday. And I got it. But, I didn't like it."

"What's not to like?"

"I didn't like the fairness of it all. Don't get me wrong. I love my success but there was always something missing. Even here, having my dream home, it's still not enough."

"What else could you possibly want?"

"Not what, but who. The thing that's always been missing is someone to share it with. Not someone who's here because of the glamour of it all, but someone who loves me for me. Like, someone who knew me before the fame. Someone like the amazing, sexy, smart, talented Riley Cavanaugh."

"I'm really not that special. Just ask Brad."

"The hell you aren't. He's an asshole for not realizing what he had with you."

"Right. If I'm so wonderful, why did he think nothing of throwing me away like a piece of garbage?" She grumbles.

"I honestly have no idea. You're by far the most intriguing woman I've ever known. I thought I knew everything there was to know about you, but I was wrong. The woman who's spent these first two days driving me absolutely wild is something I never expected."

"Well, she's always been there somewhere. Just that nobody ever let her come out and play. Until now."

Before I get a chance to say another word, she's on top of me. I watch, drooling, as she slowly lifts her top off and tosses it aside. Her naked breasts look even more incredible in the moonlight. I want her so damn bad, I can taste it. She quickly strips me naked. My dick's standing at full attention as she runs her hands all over my chest. I slide her bottoms and panties off, loving the feeling of her warm skin.

Still straddling me, she lowers her head and crushes her lips to mine. I feel her tongue in my mouth. All I can think about is having my dick inside her. She moves her lips to my neck then drags her tongue across my throat and down my chest. I'm aching to feel her wrapped around me, but she's still using her tongue on me. I watch her lick down my abs as she moans. I can't take another second of this sweet torture.

"Please, baby, I need to be inside you. NOW!"

"My, my. Eager aren't we."

She ignores my begging and moves down to my inner thighs. She sucks them one at a time and I just about blow my load on the spot. Damn, this woman is trying to kill me. Finally, she slides back up my body and takes me inside her. I watch in awe as she slides up and down my dick, her sexy tits bouncing like crazy. I let out a deep growl when she leans forward and starts sucking my neck. Everything this woman does drives me crazy.

"Oh baby, you feel so good. Ride me hard baby. I love how incredible your pussy feels."

She rides me faster and harder until I fill her. She keeps riding until her body quakes and she screams. She collapses on my chest and kisses me with more passion than anything I've ever felt. That's all it takes and I'm hard again. I'm still inside her, so I roll us over until she's on her back. She wraps her legs around my waist as I fuck her.

"Oh Ace, harder baby. You feel so damn good inside me. Mmmm...baby."

I keep up my hard and fast pace until again I empty inside her. She follows close behind, shaking even harder this time. She screams so loud, I think they heard her in the next county. I lie next to her and pull her close. We're both drenched in sweat, chests heaving from the most incredible sex I've ever had.

"Damn, woman, I think I need a dip in the pool to cool off. Care to join me?"

"Damn right, let's go Mr. Sexy."

We get in the pool and the water feels amazing. She splashes me and takes off, but I quickly catch her and pull her into an embrace. She tries to wiggle away but when she can't, she moves her hands to my ass and squeezes me hard. Damn she's naughty. She starts tickling my sides. We're laughing hysterically, holding each other tight as the water cools our skin.

I lift her up into my arms and she wraps hers around my neck. I kiss her tenderly and sit her down on the edge of the pool. She grabs two towels for us to dry off. I climb out and take one. After we're dry, we get back in our pajamas and again lay in the grass to stargaze. Everything feels different now that we've said those words. Different in a good way, though. She lets out a big yawn. No surprise after the day we had. I get up and help her up. We walk over to the tent. I zip the two sleeping bags together so I can hold her. We kiss goodnight and she quickly falls asleep. I watch her for a few minutes. That's the last thing I remember until the sun lights up our tent the next morning.

CHAPTER 5
Riley

* * *

I'm awakened by the sound of an acoustic guitar. I sit up and see Ace sitting next to me, quietly strumming. I slide over and lay my head on his shoulder while he continues playing. From the first time he ever picked up a guitar, I knew he was special. The man never took one single lesson. He would listen to a song and just start playing it. We would sit up in his bedroom for hours, me just listening to him play all our favorite songs. I tear up at the memory, still in shock at what these last two days have brought me. I hear him stop playing.

"Doll, is everything okay?"

"Yes, sorry. These are happy tears. I was thinking about how you used to play guitar for me in your room."

He pulls me in close and says, "How are you really, though, after what Brad did?"

"Brad who? Seriously, though, I really am okay and that's all thanks to you. In just two short days, you've reminded me that I'm just as much a person as anyone else. Not to mention the holy-shit-that-was-incredible pleasure you've been giving me. I don't know if you ever knew, but I secretly had a crush on you pretty much from middle school on."

"I had no idea. I must confess something. You weren't the only one hiding their feelings. I was always interested in being more than friends. I never said anything because I didn't know if you felt the same way. I was afraid that if you didn't, it would hurt our friendship. I knew I didn't want you out of my life, so I kept it quiet."

"Then why did you leave me and lose touch?"

"I'm so sorry about that, but I promise it had nothing to do with you. You remember how hard school was for us. My self-worth was at an all-time low by graduation. In my head, the only thing I could think of doing was getting out of here and starting over. I was selfish, never giving any thought to what, or more importantly, who I was leaving behind."

"You weren't selfish. I completely understand. That lack of self-confidence stayed with me. Even though I was successful at my job, I never let myself believe it. It's also why I let Brad treat me the way he did for so long. I should have sent him packing, but in my mind, I was being treated exactly the way I deserved."

"What did he do to you? And if you're not ready to tell me, I understand."

"I've never told anyone. It might help me finally move past it if I do, but I feel bad burdening you with it."

"Don't! I want to listen." He pleads.

"Okay. He never hurt me physically, but in a way, what he did was worse, at least for me. It was constant put-downs and mean-spirited comments. He didn't like the way I did anything. I remember one meal I cooked, and I was so proud of it. He took one bite, spit it on the table, and shoved the plate across the table. Food went everywhere. He screamed at me to clean it up and he stormed out to go get something to eat. He never had one nice word to say about the way I looked or anything. He left me thinking I was this hideous creature."

I pause to take a breath, then continue.

"You have no idea how close I came to not getting in that limo. Even as I rode over here, I almost had Bruce take me back home. When you thanked him and called me a beauty, I can tell you that I thought you needed your eyes examined. But you've shown me that I am actually worth something and I don't know how to thank you."

"You already have. For the first time since I left for LA, I don't feel alone. And before you say it, yes, I know I was always surrounded by people, but I was still lonely."

"How could you still feel lonely?"

"Because none of them were you, Riley."

"Oh, Ace." I smile.

"Okay, enough of this mushy stuff. What do you want to do today?"

"I really want to go somewhere. Don't get me wrong, I love your house, I just feel like a change of scenery. But, not somewhere around here."

"I have an idea. Do you trust me enough to keep it a surprise?"

"Absolutely."

"Okay. I'll be back. I need to make a couple of calls."

"I'm so excited."

"Me too, doll!"

I walk over to the bench in Ace's garden while he goes inside. I can't wait to see where he's taking me and what he has in store for me. So far, pretty much all we've done is have sex. I'm certainly not complaining, but I think a certain body part of mine needs a break! Though I suspect if he flashed me that sexy look, I'd be putty in his oh-so-capable hands. My thoughts totally go on a tangent and I start thinking about the locked door from my tour of the house. I really want to ask him about it, or even better, see it. I'm debating on whether I'm excited or scared to see what's in there. I'm so lost in thought, I don't hear Ace come back outside.

"All set, doll," he announces, as I jump out of my skin.

"I totally did not hear you come back."

"Sorry, babe. But we need to go get ready. Bruce will be here in about half an hour."

"Oh my god, we're taking the limo?"

"Damn right. My girl travels in style! Plus, with the tinted windows, nobody will see you." He winks at me.

"Can we make out while we're riding?"

"Damn, woman, is that all you think about?"

"Hell yeah, sexy."

We head up to his bedroom to pack.

"You'll need enough clothes for three days, babe."

"Okay. I can't wait to find out where we're going."

"You'll know when we get there."

After we pack, we go to Ace's living room to wait for Bruce. He arrives right on time. After he opens the door for us, he puts our bags in the trunk and we head off to our mystery destination. About two hours later, we arrive. Ace and I spent most of the ride kissing, so I never took notice of a single sign. He rolls down the window so I can look out. I squeal with delight when I see where we are.

"Oh my god, Ace, oh my god! I've wanted to come here since it opened, but dick-for-brains wouldn't bring me."

"So that means I get to pop your Hard Rock cherry!"

"Mmmm."

I look and we're sitting outside the VIP entrance. Bruce comes around and opens the door. I get out and Ace follows me. A bellhop comes over and loads our luggage. He waits for us inside. Ace arranges with Bruce when to pick us up. Once he pulls away, we walk inside. The bellhop leads us to the VIP check-in, bypassing the long line of people in the regular check-in. I'm feeling a bit spoiled. After Ace finishes checking in, the bellhop leads us to the elevator. We're on the 17th floor of the South Tower in a huge suite. My eyes go wide when I walk inside. Ace tips the bellhop then walks over to me and pulls me in close.

"Might this be to your liking, my darling?" He asks.

"Oh yes, good sir. It pleases me greatly."

"And what would my lady like to do?"

I look around. "Sorry, no lady here. Just a horny bitch," I say, laughing.

Before I realize what's happening, I'm over Ace's shoulder and on my way to the suite's bedroom. I bang on his ass like it's a pair of bongos. He puts me down on the bed and lays next to me. We quickly strip each other naked. He fucks me hard and fast, both of us quickly exploding together. I love the long, sexy sessions, but damn, those quickies are hot as hell. We grab a quick shower and get dressed.

"So, what's on the agenda?" I ask.

"I thought we could hit the casino for a while then the boardwalk. I also have something special planned for dinner."

"That sounds perfect."

We're walking around the casino when I see a sign advertising a poker tournament starting tomorrow. A well-kept secret about me is my penchant for playing online. I would really love to enter but I see it's a five-thousand dollar buy-in. I sigh loudly, knowing that's outside what I can safely spend.

"What's wrong, doll?"

Pointing at the sign, I say, "I would love to enter that."

"Wait, you play poker?"

"Yeah, I've been playing online for years. I got hooked after watching a World Series of Poker tournament on TV."

"Damn, girl, any other secrets you've been keeping?"

"That's for me to know and you to try to find out."

"Brat. Now, about the tourney. You should enter."

"I would, but that entry fee is too much for me."

"What if you had a sponsor who paid the fee?"

"A sponsor?"

"Yeah, me."

"I can't ask you to do that."

"You're not asking. Come with me."

We walk over to the area where the sign says to register. There's a casino employee named Art sitting at the table.

"May I help you?" Art asks.

"My woman would like to register for the poker tournament," Ace replies.

"Name, please," Art says.

"Riley Cavanaugh. C-a-v-a-n-a-u-g-h."

"I'll need to see your ID, ma'am," Art says.

I take out my wallet and show him my license. He nods.

"Now, there's just the matter of your entry fee."

"I'll be paying that," Ace answers and hands a credit card to Art.

Art runs the card and once it's approved, he hands a slip to Ace to sign. He then hands me a sheet with the rules and any other information.

"Good luck, ma'am," Art says, sneering.

We head back towards the casino.

"So, I see he's another asshat who thinks women can't win at poker," I say.

"Are you any good? I didn't mean that the way it sounded, just curious."

"I've won quite a few online tournaments and that's without being able to see my opponents. With this, I'll be able to watch for tells."

"Damn, who are you, Riley?"

"Time changes people." I laugh.

"Definitely for the better in your case, babe."

"You too, Ace. Now, how about some penny slots?"

"Lead the way, beautiful."

We walk around until I see a game that looks fun, called Piggy Bankin'. We sit down at two of the machines and start playing. After only a couple of spins, I hit the bonus game and end up winning a decent amount. Ace has the same good luck and after an hour, we've both got a nice total built up. We decide to cash it out before our luck changes. He puts the tickets in his wallet until we're ready to cash them in.

"What do you say we hit the boardwalk and do some people-watching?" Ace asks.

"Okay. When I was younger and my parents brought me to Ocean City, I would sit on the boardwalk and make up funny stories about all the people."

"You should be writing."

"I wrote some of them down back then, but never did anything with them. I prefer to read, especially all the smutty books."

"I like the sound of that. I'm still waiting for you to read some to me so we can act them out."

"I packed one for our trip here."

"Well, I know one thing we'll be doing then, my naughty woman."

"That bed will never be the same!"

"Who said anything about bed?"

"Oh my, Ace!"

We walk over to a bench and sit down. There's a lot of foot traffic and it's full of some very interesting characters. I feel Ace's arm move around my shoulders, so I lay my head on his shoulder. These last few days have been the happiest I've ever experienced. I can only imagine what the rest of our time together is going to be like. Ace's voice interrupts my daydream.

"Let's head back inside. I have a couple of surprises before dinner."

We head back inside and walk over to the South Tower elevators. Ace presses the button for 3 instead of our floor.

"Where are we going?" I ask.

"This is the first of your many surprises, my doll."

We reach the third floor and step out. I see a sign pointing to the hotel spa. Ace takes my hand as we walk to the Rock Spa & Salon. We're immediately greeted by a woman named Jasmine.

"Right this way, Mr. London, Miss Cavanaugh," Jasmine says.

She leads us to a private room with two massage tables next to each other.

"Enjoy your couples' massage. Make yourselves comfortable on the tables. Your masseuses will be in shortly."

Jasmine leaves, closing the door behind her. I've never had a massage before and I'm a little nervous, so I just stand there staring at Ace. He points at the towels hanging on the wall.

"Just strip down, lie face down on the table and cover that sexy ass with the towel," he says, showing me those sexy dimples.

"Thanks. Sorry I'm so dumb."

"Stop that, woman!"

I get comfortable on the table and watch Ace strip down and lie on the table next to me, I need another towel to wipe the drool off my chin. I hear a knock on the door and Ace tells them to come in. A man and woman enter the room to give us our massages. Ace and I hold hands and gaze into each other's eyes the entire time. Once the massages are over, the two employees leave the room so we can get dressed.

"Thank you for this. I really needed it," I say.

"My pleasure, doll."

"It will be later."

"I like the sound of that. Now off to your next surprise. Come with me."

Ace walks me to the salon and we're again greeted by Jasmine.

"Our expert Marco will be joining us shortly," she tells us. "Miss Cavanaugh, please have a seat." Jasmine points to the end chair.

I sit down while Ace follows her out of the salon. What else does he have planned for me? I'm sitting for a few minutes when Marco comes in. He looks at me from several angles before he walks over to the chair.

"Oh yes, I can work with this. You're already beautiful. I'll make you stunning," Marco says.

"Thank you," I respond.

An hour later, I look in the mirror and a new and improved Riley looks back at me. My dark brown hair now has golden highlights and is about six inches shorter. The style really suits my face. For the first time in a long time, I feel good about how I look. A few minutes later, Ace comes back into the salon and I hear a loud whistle escape his lips.

"You're stunning. Marco, wow."

Marco smiles as he walks out of the room. Ace takes my hand and walks me down the hall where Jasmine is standing outside yet another room. She takes me inside and I see a rack of evening gowns and a few closed cases. I can't believe my eyes.

"She's in good hands, Mr. London," Jasmine says as she whisks me into the room and closes the door. "Time to knock that man's pants off," Jasmine says.

I try on several dresses before I find the one. The dress is emerald green satin. The material feels amazing against my skin and I force myself to admit that I look great. The dress shows just enough of my cleavage that Ace is going to drool. The slit in the dress shows off my left leg with each step I take. We settle on black shoes with a low heel.

"Time now for accessories. Mr. London has spared no expense," Jasmine says.

By the time we're done, I have a tiara, emerald earrings and a matching diamond bracelet and necklace. I feel like a princess. All of a sudden a wave of something I can't describe washes over me, and I need to sit down. Jasmine rushes over.

"Are you okay, miss?" She asks.

"I can't do this. I don't deserve to be treated like this."

"If I may, can I offer some advice, ma'am?"

"Please."

"Someone made you feel this way and whoever that someone is, they are dead wrong. No man does all of this for a woman unless she's someone very special. Embrace the woman that you are,I see the way Mr. London looks at you. There's a hunger in his eyes."

"Thank you so much for saying that."

"One more piece of advice. Go commando tonight. He'll worship you for it, if you know what I mean," she says with a wink.

"Oh, I do know. Thank you for everything today."

"It was my pleasure. Now, let's wrap everything up so he's surprised when he sees you tonight."

Jasmine walks me out to the front, where Ace is waiting for me. He takes care of paying for everything and leaves a tip for everyone who helped today. We walk to the elevator to head up to our room. We shower together but I won't allow him to see me get ready. It's my turn to surprise him. I take Jasmine's advice and only put a bra on. The girls are a bit too big to go commando upstairs. Downstairs on the other hand, well, he'll have easy access.

Once I get my dress and shoes on, I put on the tiara and jewelry. I'm starting to feel nervous again, but I take a deep breath and remember what Jasmine said to me. I peek out and see Ace standing there in a white suit with a navy blue shirt and I almost pass out cold. He looks incredible. I can't bring myself to come out of the room. Damn that fuckosaurus rex ex-boyfriend for doing this to me.

"I'm ready," I say quietly.

"Well, then, come out here and let me see you, doll."

I walk out and see Ace's jaw drop.

"I look that bad?" I ask.

"You're fucking stunning, woman. Holy shit."

I feel my cheeks get hot as Ace eyes me up and down. He licks his lips and my breath hitches in my throat. I start thinking about his hands on me. Wait until he finds out I'm not wearing panties. But, that will be my secret until later.

"Where are we headed?" I ask.

"You'll find out, baby. Shall we?"

"Yes, please. Are you sure this isn't too much? Jasmine said I needed the accessories."

"Doll, it's perfect."

I smile as Ace holds out his arm. I link my arm through his and we head to the elevators. He leads me across the casino floor to the board-walk exit. I look out and see a portion of the beach closed off with red velvet ropes. A long red carpet leads to the ropes. I look inside the ropes and see a small iron table and two chairs.

We walk down the beach entrance and cross the carpet. When we get closer, I see a silver bucket with a bottle sticking out and two glasses. A waiter moves the rope aside, allowing us to enter. We sit down at the table and the waiter pours us each a glass of champagne. He lets us know our dinner will be served shortly and heads back inside.

"What's for dinner?" I ask.

"A seafood feast."

"That sounds delicious."

"Not as delicious as you in that dress."

"Thank you."

A few minutes later, a group of waiters comes by with a small table and a couple trays of food. I see shrimp, crab legs, and lobster tails, along with rice and asparagus. My stomach starts growling. I can't wait to dig into some crab legs. One of the waiters hands us bibs with lobsters on them to protect our clothing while we eat. I start with a snow crab cluster, one of my favorites.

"Baby, watching you eat and handle those crab legs is getting me hot."

"Is there anything that doesn't get you hot, Mr. Hornypants?"

He smiles but doesn't say a word. I have a feeling we're gonna have some fun later. After we finish eating, we clean up our hands with the wipes we were provided. The moon and the sun have swapped places. The night sky is clear so all the stars are visible. The moon's reflection off the ocean is beautiful. The waiters return and clear everything away. They hand a bag to Ace, then return to the hotel.

Ace grabs a blanket out of the bag and spreads it out. "Come lay with me, please, baby." he says.

I lay down and he takes me into his arms, kissing me hard. His tongue in my mouth gets me wet. He runs a hand up my leg and under my dress. When he finds my little surprise, he breaks the kiss and just stares at me.

"My naughty, naughty woman."

I'm about to respond when he moves between my legs. I feel his tongue between my folds and I moan loudly. He quickly sends me over the edge with his powerful tongue. We spend the next several hours fucking on the beach until we're both completely exhausted. We get dressed and return to our suite. We get undressed and crawl into bed naked. I don't remember much after Ace turned off the light and kissed me goodnight.

CHAPTER 6

Ace

* * *

I wake up in the morning and I'm alone in bed. I walk out and see Riley sitting at the table in the living room with her laptop open.

"What'cha doin', babe?" I ask her.

"I woke up and couldn't fall back to sleep. I decided to use the time to play some online poker to make sure my skills are sharp for today."

"I can't wait to watch you in action."

"I'm nervous and excited all at the same time. I do have a slight advantage in that men tend not to take women seriously. If they underestimate me, it will work in my favor."

"We need to get you fueled up. Hardrock Cafe for breakfast?"

"Sounds good!"

I take her hand as we ride down to the casino floor. We walk over to the cafe and get seated. We order breakfast and coffee.

"Still good, doll?"

"I am, but could I ask a favor?"

"Anything, baby."

"After breakfast, can we take a walk on the beach before I have to sign in? The ocean will calm me so I can stay focused for the game."

"Your wish is my command."

She smiles at me and my insides turn to mush. I love this woman more than I ever knew was possible, but I can never tell her. After we finish breakfast, I pay the check, Riley's quiet as we walk to the exit for the beach so I don't say anything. I know she's trying to get herself in the right mindset for the tournament. I put an arm around her as we walk, smiling when I feel her lay her head on my shoulder. After we've walked for a bit, she sits down. I join her and return my arm to her shoulders, as again her head finds my shoulder. I wish I could freeze this moment.

About half an hour before the tournament check in opens, we walk back into the casino and over to the table. I stand in line with Riley and start scoping out her competition. She's the only woman in line so far. I see some of the other men looking at her with smirks on their faces. Little do they know she's no slouch and she certainly isn't stupid. But, like she said, best to let them think she is.

When it's her turn to check in, I see my first glimpse of my woman in action. A casino employee is sitting at the table checking in all the players.

"Name, please," he says to Riley.

"Riley Catacombs." She giggles. "I mean, Riley Cavanaugh. I forgot my last name for a second."

I try my damnedest not to react. I watch everyone else standing in line and most of them are laughing and gesturing at her, She pretends not to notice any of it. I watch her plaster a dopey grin on her face. They point her to the right and she starts to turn left, gives another giggle then heads the right way. I hear one of the men say he hopes he's at her table so he knows he won't be the first one eliminated. Be careful what you wish for, asshole, I think to myself.

We get into the room and there's two signs separated by a rope. One sends spectators to their seating area and the other sends players to the tables. There's a line of competitors waiting so I decide to help her out a bit. Before I head over to the seating area, I give her a quick kiss.

"Good luck, Riley. Don't forget, you're playing poker, not your favorite game, Go Fish," I say.

Not missing a beat, she replies, "I am? Oh no, did I sign up for the wrong tournament again? Oh well, guess I'll play anyway."

She flashes me the slightest smile then heads to the players area, so I lose sight of her. I take a seat in the front row so I have a good view of her while she's playing. I can't wait to see her make an ass out of those jerks. About half an hour later, poker legend Phil Hellmuth walks out to the area where the tables are set up. Riley must be freaking out, as she told me he's the one who got her hooked on Texas Hold 'Em.

"Welcome to today's tournament, everyone. The games will begin shortly. Our players are finding out their table assignments as we speak. As players start to get eliminated, we'll combine tables until we have our final nine players. Those nine players will get a small break then the final table will begin. We'll continue until one player remains. That player will win our grand prize of one hundred thousand dollars. And here come our players now."

Phil stands and waits for everyone to be seated and set their chip stacks how they want them. Once each table has a dealer, he turns his microphone back on.

"Best of luck to all our players. There's only one thing left to say. Shuffle up and deal!"

It doesn't take long for some of the less-skilled players to get eliminated. I watch the big screens set up and see Riley pretend to not know what she was doing for a couple of hands, just to lull her competitors into a false sense of security. Since then, she's already forced two men all-in and eliminated them.

Several hours pass and nine tables have now dwindled down to two. Of course, my woman's still playing and she's currently sitting in third place in terms of chip count. A couple more hours pass and the final table is set. Most of the spectators have gone and I'm guessing those remaining are family and friends of the final nine. Phil again comes to the floor.

"We have our final table. The players will take a 15 minute break then we'll get started. May the best man or woman win." Phil says to the remaining crowd.

The players return and are assigned seats. Riley has her back to me, which is probably better for her concentration. I sit and watch as player after player eventually busts out and only the top three remain, Riley has moved into second place, only about 1000 chips less than the first place player. The third place player only has about one-quarter the chips of my woman. He only makes it a few hands before Riley puts him all-in and finishes him off with queens full of aces.

Riley's opponent's name is Jason. Riley and Jason are seated at opposite ends of the table, across from the dealer. It only takes a few hands for Riley to overtake the chip lead. From there, she's a force to be reckoned with, and about 90 minutes in, she has Jason all-in. If he pulls this out, it will deliver a serious blow to her chip stack. He turns over kings full of aces and everyone gasps. There's only three hands that beat his. Because of his high cards, she can't tie him. All eyes are on the screen, waiting for Riley to show her hand. I jump out of my seat when I see four queens appear on the screen.

"You did it, baby," I scream out.

Jason walks over and shakes Riley's hand, as Phil returns one more time to wrap things up.

"I'd like to congratulate both players for surviving until the end. But, there can only be one winner. This year's tournament is one for the history books, as we have our first female champion, Riley Cavanaugh," Phil says as he tips the microphone toward my girl.

"Thank you so much. I can't believe this is real."

Phil presents her with her trophy and her prize money as I walk down. I grab her and twirl her around in my arms. There's a small reception in the back of the room, so she and I walk back. This is the most confident I've ever seen her and I couldn't be prouder of my badass woman. We walk over to where Phil is standing.

"I need to give you an extra special thank you for this," she says to him.

"Why is that?"

"You're the reason I got hooked on poker. I was home watching The World Series of Poker back in 1989. After seeing what you did in that tournament, I started playing."

"Thank you for saying that and for watching. That was an amazing year for me."

"I can't even imagine the excitement of winning that level of tourney."

"It's definitely a feeling like no other."

"I hope I'm not overstepping, but would you be willing to sign my registration paper?" She asks.

"My pleasure."

As Phil was signing her paper, a casino employee approaches to grab Phil, Riley, and Jason for a couple of pictures. They take her email address as she'll be sent copies. We will definitely be framing those. After the reception ends, we're given an escort to our room because of the prize money, which we lock in the room safe. It's almost one in the morning when we're finally back in our room.

"Baby, I'm so proud of you. Those dudes never knew what hit 'em. The irony of it wasn't lost on me."

"What do you mean?"

"Babe, you beat his three kings with four queens! Just like my queen beat all those kings."

"In the excitement of it all, I didn't even think about that. Right now, though, all I can think about is my head on that pillow."

"Me too."

We get ready for bed and crawl under the covers together. I pull her in tight and kiss her goodnight. She's quickly sound asleep in my arms, and that's the last thing I remember.

CHAPTER 7

Riley

* * *

I'm awakened the next morning by lips sucking on my neck and something hard poking me in the ass.

"Good morning, Mr. Horny." I tease.

"Good morning, poker queen.," Ace responds.

Before I realize what's happening I'm somehow out of my pajamas and he's on top of me. We enjoy a quick, hard fuck then get up and shower. We're heading back home today, but I don't mind. I'm still flying high from my exciting tournament win. We decided to cut the trip a day early before anyone found out what room we were staying in, given the prize money in our safe. Once we're dressed and packed, Ace calls for a bellhop. The concierge also sends a guard to escort us to the lobby. I see Bruce standing outside the limo when we're escorted outside.

"Congratulations, Miss Cavanaugh," Bruce says once we're inside the car.

"Thank you so much," I respond.

He smiles then starts the drive back to Ace's house. After he drops us off, I ask Ace for a favor, since I don't have my car here.

"Would you mind driving me to the bank so I can deposit this?" I ask.

"Of course. I have an idea for today's adventure when we're done. What bank are you with?"

"The one on Main Street."

"My suggestion is we call and make an appointment to handle the deposit privately, given the amount."

"Good idea. Give me a moment to call."

I hang up and let Ace know they have availability now, so we head out to Ace's garage. He hadn't shown me the garage during our tour. My jaw drops when I see what's inside. I gasp when I see it.

"Oh my god! A 1957 Ford Fairlane in official Flame Red. And it's a convertible!" I squeal.

"Wait, you know cars? Where did that come from?"

"My grandpa had one. I absolutely loved it. He taught me to drive in that car."

"You're in luck, as that's what we're taking today."

"Yay!" I exclaim, bouncing and clapping.

Ace puts Sirius XM's Hair Nation on and we start driving to the bank. He parks as close as he can and holds me tight as I clutch the brief-case tight. I let one of the tellers know I have an appointment, so she calls the bank manager and he comes out to get us.

"Good afternoon. My name is William. What can I do for you today?"

I give William a short version of how I got the money and that I wanted to deposit it. We discuss some options. I end up putting half into my savings account and investing the remaining amount. Once we finish all the necessary paperwork, William hands me my receipts and copies of the papers, then walks us back to the lobby.

"Thank you for your business, Miss Cavanaugh. Enjoy the rest of your afternoon." William says.

"Thank you, sir." I respond.

We walk out to Ace's car, but he walks to the passenger's side and tosses me the keys. My jaw drops. I can't believe he's letting me drive.

"Are you sure?" I ask in disbelief.

"You bet, doll. Let's see what you can do."

"You know I can handle a stick, babe."

"Yes, ma'am, I sure as hell do." he laughs.

I drive us to a diner we used to eat in all the time when we were in high school. After we finish lunch, he takes over driving. He takes us down some country roads and there's no other traffic for miles, so he floors it. The wind blowing through my hair feels amazing, as we both sing at the top of our lungs. We drive for another couple of hours.

"Would you like to stop for some dinner?" Ace asks.

"I'd love to."

We drive for another hour when I spot a cute little outdoor café.

"Can we stop here?" I ask.

Ace pulls into the parking lot and we walk inside. We both order a burger, fries, and a chocolate milkshake. We enjoy our dinner and even more, each other's company. We spend a couple of hours at the café, laughing and talking. I'm having some strong feelings for him, but I'm not sure if it's real or just me trying to deal with the pain my ex-fuckface caused me, so I don't say anything. After we leave the cafe, Ace starts driving back to his house. We're about a half-hour away from his house when he pulls into a scenic overlook and parks the car.

"I thought we could watch the sunset together before we head back to my house." he says.

"That sounds perfect."

"How about we climb into the backseat?"

"Mmmm, naughty..." I tease.

We climb in the backseat. Ace puts his arms around me and I rest my head on his shoulder as we watch the sun descend. The colors are breathtaking, thought not quite as breathtaking as the man holding me. Once the sun was out of sight, we got back into the front seat and finished the drive home.

Once we were inside, Ace asked, "Would you like to get a snack?"

"Yes, I'm hungry."

With the naughty gleam in his eye, he replied, "Me too, baby."

Ace pulled her into his arms again. I could really get used to this man holding me in those sexy, muscular arms.

"Baby, we've had some pretty incredible sex so far, but there are some new positions I'd love to try."

"Yes, please, my sexy rock god."

We ride the elevator to his bedroom and we were naked in record speed. We lay down in bed and Ace flashes me the naughtiest smile I've ever seen.

"Did I ever tell you what my favorite number is?" he asked.

"No, but I am curious!"

Not at all surprisingly, Ace responded, "69."

I feel a sensation run through my stomach and my heart starts pounding in my chest.

"I wanna do that with you. Come sit on my face and wrap that pretty mouth around my cock."

"But..."

"But what, woman?"

"I'm afraid I'll hurt you."

"Stop that, woman. Now get on my face so I can taste that sweet pussy."

I crawl over to Ace and straddle his head. I feel his tongue on my pussy and I moan. I lower my head and wrap my mouth around his hot dick. Fuck, he tastes so good. I feel his fingers slide in and out of me while he drives me wild with his tongue. I hear him growling as he pleasures me. I tease his balls with my fingers while I suck him hard. My entire body quakes as I start to come undone. He fingers me harder and I explode on his face.

"Fuck, woman, that was hot." he says as he empties into my mouth.

I climb off and face him so he can see me swallow him. I lick my lips and he growls again. I've never done that before and I didn't know what I was missing.

"Now, woman, I wanna be inside you. Get on your knees and lower your chest to the bed."

I do as I'm told.

"Good girl. Now, get ready for a pounding like you've never felt."

I emit something that sounds like a tigress growling as Ace grabs my waist. I feel his dick slide into my pussy hard and fast. I feel him smack my ass while he fucks me. Feeling bold, I turn things up a notch and tease my clit with my finger.

"Damn, woman, that's fuckin' hot." He quickly empties inside me, groaning loudly. "On your back. NOW!"

I lay on my back.

"I want to watch you pleasure yourself. Spread those legs and let me see that sweet pussy. Now, get those fingers working."

I start teasing my clit as I watch Ace licking his lips. He suddenly grabs his dick and starts pumping. Holy shit, he's so turned on watching me that he's hard again. He pulls me on top of him and I wrap my pussy around his dick. Unlike the hard, fast fuck he gave me, I'm going to make this last. I slide up and down slowly, savoring each stroke. His hands explore my back as we experience the intense passion. This time, we come together as he pulls me down and holds me tight.

He rolls me onto my back and again he enters me. We spend the next hour with our bodies connected in the most intense pleasure I've ever felt. By the time we were done, we were both starving. We didn't even bother to get dressed. We rode the elevator downstairs and went to the kitchen to grab some junk food. I grabbed a box of Lucky Charms while Ace opted for popcorn.

We got into bed and turned on a movie. Ace took one of each marshmallow out of the box and ate them off my stomach, both of us laughing. Once the movie was over, Ace turned everything off and pulled the covers over us. The last thing I remember was him pulling me close and kissing me goodnight.

CHAPTER 8

Ace

* * *

"Baby, it's time to wake up."

I watch her sit up slowly and rub her eyes. I'm standing next to the bed, still in my pajamas.

"But Ace, it's still dark outside."

"I know, doll, but I have something special planned for today. We need to hurry though."

She jumps up when I flash her a smile. I take her hand and lead her to the elevator. When we're downstairs, I take her out to the backyard and watch her jaw drop. She does that a lot! I snuck out of bed while she was out cold and set up an open tent. I put an air mattress inside, covered with a large blanket. I also have another blanket on the ground outside of the tent.

"What is all this?" she asks.

"I have a lot in store for you today, but first come lay with me. I want to watch the sunrise with you in my arms."

We lay on the blanket outside the tent and gaze at the sky. I can't get enough of this woman. She feels so right in my arms. I just wish I had the courage to tell her I was falling for her. But, we agreed, this would be a ten-day staycation. I will, however, make sure she forgets all about the ass who put her in this situation. I can't fight the urge to kiss her, so I crush my lips to hers and joined my tongue with hers. I kept her in my arms until the sun had fully risen.

"Go have a seat at the table. Breakfast will be served shortly." I say.

"Mmmm, yummy. I'm starving!" she says, batting her eyes at me. There goes my dick stirring again. Shit, this woman drives me crazy!

I head inside to cook breakfast for us. I return a little while later carrying two plates. I run back inside and grab two cups of coffee then join her at the table. I watch Riley wolf down her food until her plate is clean. I love watching a woman who's not afraid to eat. When we're done, I stand and hold out my hand to her. She takes my hand and stands too. I take her into the tent.

"Baby, get undressed and lie on your front."

I watch as all her sexy flesh appears. I remove my shirt then grab the bag I have in the corner of the tent. I pull out a bottle of edible massage oil.

"Since this is your vacation, you deserve some pampering today. How would you like a sensual massage?" I ask.

"Mmm, yes please. I long to feel your strong hands on me."

I smile as I put a little bit of the oil on her back and start massaging it in. I move to her shoulders and neck, as she emits soft moans. I work my way down to her sexy round ass and spend quite a bit of time there. I run my hands up and down each of her shapely legs and gently spread them. Fuck, this woman is beautiful.

"Lay on your back, doll."

I start my journey back up her incredible body. I massage the insides of her thighs and she starts writhing. I can only imagine the effect this is having on my favorite part of her. But for now, I ignore it. I have plenty in store for that part later. I massage her stomach before moving to her luscious breasts. I can't take it another second and I lower my mouth on one breast then the other, sucking hard.

I run my tongue between them then down her body, stopping just short of the spot I most want to taste. I can tell she wants it too, the way her body is writhing. I move down and suck the inside of each thigh.

"Oh, fuck, Ace, so good, baby." she cries out.

"Where should I lick next?"

"Please, baby, my pussy. I'm throbbing for you."

I decide to torture her a bit, so I suck her thighs again, harder this time. Her body bucks off the bed. She grabs my hair and tries to pull my mouth up to her pussy.

"Behave, baby, or you won't get what you want."

She lays perfectly still.

"That's my good girl. Get ready for your reward."

I slide my hands under her ass and lift her up to my mouth. I run my tongue slowly between her folds as her fingers run through my hair.

"Doll, I wanna hear you let loose and talk dirty to me while I pleasure you. I better enjoy it or no more tongue inside those sweet folds."

I watch her lock eyes with me. "Oh fuck, Ace. I love the way your hot tongue feels on my pussy. Please, baby, suck my fuckin' clit. Mmmm, yes, like that."

"More baby. Filthier than you've ever talked to anyone. Tell me your secret desires, doll."

"Fuck, Ace, please, spank my pussy. Please, god, make me fuckin' squirt."

"Holy shit, woman."

She takes her fingers and spreads herself wide. Damn, that's the prettiest pussy I've ever seen. I give her a couple light swats on her mound.

"Harder, please, baby."

I spank her a little harder then slide a couple fingers inside her. I find and stroke her g-spot hard, as she screams. I lower my head and suck her clit hard, while I keep fucking her with my fingers. Her entire body convulses as she comes hard, drenching my hand and my face with her sweet juices. I run my tongue up and down her slit, tasting as much of her orgasm as I can, and fuck, she tastes incredible. My cock is harder than it's ever been.

"Baby, come with me to the hot tub."

Her legs are shaking from her orgasm, so I help her up and carry her. I sit down in the hot tub and motion her to climb onto my lap. She grabs my dick and takes me inside. She bounces up and down on my dick as water splashes everywhere. I cannot get enough of her hot pussy wrapped around me. She feels like heaven. I hold her tight as she moves on top of me until we come together. I have to bite her shoulder to keep from telling her I love her.

Riley climbs off and sits down next to me. I turn on the jets and we sit and relax. I put an arm around her and pull her in close. We sit quietly for a while, basking in the afterglow of more incredible sex while the jets massage our bodies. I hear the softest snores as she falls asleep on my shoulder. I can't stand the thought of ever spending another day without her. I can't believe this is the second half of our time together. What am I going to do without her? I put that aside and just focus on the time we have left.

My mind starts wandering to the room I never showed her. I saw her looking at the door when I was showing her around, but she never said anything. I think I may have to unlock that door on her last day here. I was afraid to show her then , as I wasn't sure how she would react. She has since shown her dirty side, so maybe she can handle it. She stirs awake, snapping me out of my reverie.

"I'm starving after that workout. Mind if I make some lunch for us?" she asks.

"Not at all, under one condition." I reply.

"Oh, and what might that be?"

"I want you to stay naked. I want to watch your sexy body while you cook for me."

"Umm, okay. I guess I won't be cooking bacon, then," I tease.

"How about instead of cooking, we take it back to our youth?"

"Ooh, peanut butter and grape jelly?"

"Yeah, with chips on it!"

"Of course!"

I watch her make the sandwiches. Suddenly, she turns around with a silly look on her face. She points at her naked breasts and I lose it. She has peanut butter on one and jelly on the other. I walk over and lick each one clean. We both laugh hysterically then grab our lunch and head back out to the tent. After we eat, we hit the pool for a swim. When we're done, we get out and dry off then take a nap inside the tent. We end up sleeping until dinnertime.

Riley is still asleep, so I go inside for a few minutes to order food and dessert for us. When the food arrives, I set things up on the table and wake my woman up. We enjoy a nice meal and dessert together, as we polish off a bottle of wine. After dinner, I turn some music on and we dance naked in the backyard. It's getting hard not to tell Riley that I love her, but I manage to fight it.

We spend the rest of the night having more incredible sex as the sun goes down and the moon replaces it in the night sky. We don't stop until we're both depleted of energy. We lay down on the air mattress and I cover us with the blanket. I pull her into my arms.

"I hope you enjoyed today's activities." I smile sleepily.

"I enjoyed today more than words could say. Thank you so much."

"It was my pleasure, baby. Or should I say it was our pleasure?"

"Mmm, so much pleasure..." she said as she drifted off to sleep.

CHAPTER 9
Riley

* * *

I stir awake, wrapped in the strong, sexy arms of my man. I can hear him snoring behind me, so I lay there and just listen. I hate the thought that this fantasy has to end. Getting back to my boring reality is going to suck balls. I feel him nuzzle my neck so I turn to face him.

"Good morning," I whisper.

"Good morning, beautiful. What would you like to do today?"

"I have a few things. Having a hard time picking."

"Tell me."

"I love checking out antique shops, but I also would love to go to Baltimore for the day. I love the aquarium, plus I have a favorite restaurant there."

"Which restaurant?"

"Phillips Seafood."

"You have good taste, woman."

"Thanks. Having a hard time deciding which one I want to do." I sigh.

"Why choose? Let's do both."

"Really? But, that's a lot."

"This is your vacation and I want you to enjoy it. We can look for antique shops on our drive. Then we can tour the aquarium and have dinner at Phillips."

"I love that idea. Thank you so much for making this so amazing."

"Anything for you, doll. I was thinking we could stay overnight and drive home in the morning."

"Wow, you're really spoiling me."

"It's fun having someone to share all of this with." He smiles.

"Yes it is."

The only difference is, he'll get to keep living like this, while I go back to being boring old Riley. But, I won't let that dampen my mood today. We clean everything up from outside, head up to the shower and get ready for another fun road trip. Ace decides on his brand new red Mustang for this trip. The car is a stunning red, and I love riding with the windows open, wind blowing through my hair.

The ride to Baltimore is normally about two hours, but with stopping at several antique shops, we arrive about five hours later. We're staying at the Hilton in the inner harbor, in the Presidential Parlor. The room is stunning and even has a gorgeous view of Camden Yards. I feel like a princess. I have a feeling that the bed is going to see some action later!

After we drop off our luggage, we walk over to the aquarium. The last time we were here was in sixth grade for a school field trip. It was fun touring it with him as adults this time. We held hands the entire time, as if we were two people in love. Thinking about that was making me a little sad, but I couldn't let him know that, so I kept a smile plastered on my face.

We walked around the rest of the inner harbor, checking out shops and other attractions before heading to Phillips. Ace was able to get us the chef's table as the owner was a huge fan of his. I could get used to being a VIP everywhere I went. This is a far cry from the life I've grown accustomed to. We enjoy an indulgent meal and decadent dessert. We decide to take another walk around the harbor before heading back to the hotel.

"I'm gonna go down to the indoor pool and try to swim off some of the calories I consumed at dinner," I say. "Care to join me?"

"I'd love to. I guess we'll actually have to put swimsuits on this time." he laughs.

"Uh, yeah, I don't think they would appreciate us being naked."

"We can do that part later. That bed is going to see some shit tonight!"

I shudder with anticipation of what that sexy man has in store for my body tonight. I'm not sure I'll ever be able to be with another man again, without comparing him to Ace London! I get changed into my swimsuit then pull on a pair of shorts and sneakers. We grab towels then head to the pool. I'm happy to see nobody else is there, so I'll be able to get some good laps in.

We lay our towels on one of the lounge chairs around the pool, along with our shorts and shoes. I climb in the shallow end, and Ace follows. I quickly swim away from him, but he catches me and pulls me into an embrace.

"Behave yourself, dude, or you don't get the goods tonight." I tease.

"Well, well, Miss Feisty!"

I laugh and swim away, but he's hot on my heels. I go underwater and tug his swim shorts down then swim away. He fixes them then comes after me.

"And you told me to behave? What about you, doll? That was naughty!"

"What was naughty?"

"Yanking my trunks down."

"I did no such thing!"

"Doll! You did too!"

"You can't prove it!" I say as I splash him in the face.

"You're in trouble now, woman."

He grabs me, picks me up, and lightly tosses me back into the water. I splash him again and swim away. He catches up and we start a massive splash fight, both of us laughing until our stomachs hurt. He turns serious, pulls me in close, and lays a kiss on me that I'm surprised didn't cause my swimsuit to fall off.

"Baby, what do you say we go hit a club?" Ace asks.

"I'd love to, but I didn't bring a dress."

"You won't need one. We're going to Angels Rock Bar, so jeans and a t-shirt is perfect."

"I've heard about that place and how awesome it is. I never thought I'd get the chance to actually go."

We get back to the room and start getting ready. We grab quick showers to wash off all the chlorine. I give my hair a quick blow-dry, do my makeup, and get dressed. Once we're both ready, Ace books a rideshare service to take us to the bar. There's a line waiting to get in, so Ace grabs his phone and sends a text. A few minutes later, a man comes out and escorts us inside.

"Ace London! I can't believe you're here!" the man says.

"It's been a long time, dude. Babe, meet Jason Williams, owner of this awesome establishment. We go way back, as my band used to play here when we first started out. Jay, this is my woman, Riley." Ace says.

"Nice to meet you, Jay." I say.

"Likewise," Jay responds. "Now, let me take you to our VIP section."

We follow Jay to a section near the stage and dance floor. He removes the reserved sign from one of the empty tables and motions for us to take a seat. He leaves a menu and lets us know a waitress will be over shortly. We each order a drink and I look around while we wait. I hear some catcalls and whistles on the other side of the dance floor.

I look over and see the three most beautiful women I've ever seen. You can tell right away that they're best friends. Each of them is carrying the same designer bag, in different colors. One of them has a pink bag, one has a yellow bag, and one has a black bag. They're all wearing bikinis that leave very little to the imagination. All eyes are on them as they dance.

Motioning toward the women, I ask Ace, "wouldn't you rather be with them?"

"Babe, I won't lie, they're pretty, but I only have eyes for my woman. Let's go dance."

We walk to the dance floor. Ace puts his hands on my hips and I sway them. The "fun girls" as I've named them, join us. Ace steps aside as I dance with them, the four of us having a blast together. They told me their names are Sierra, Lacey, and Jazz. We ended up following each other on social media. Everyone should be lucky enough to have those three as friends. When we're done dancing, Ace and I return to the table and down a couple of drinks. We're just finishing another round when Jay drops by our table.

"Could I trouble you to hit the stage for a song or two? It isn't often we get someone your caliber in here." Jay asks.

"It would be my honor." Ace replies.

He follows Jay, so I'm alone at the table. Sierra, Lacey, and Jazz come join me.

"You're so lucky to be here with Ace!" Sierra says.

"I sure am. He's so hot." I reply.

When Ace comes on with the house band, Jazz says, "Come on, girl, get out there and shake your ass for that sexy man."

The girls pull me out to the dance floor. Jay escorts us to the front of the stage so we have the best view. Ace kicks ass up on stage. His voice is still as incredible as the first time I heard him sing. He does three songs with the band before he rejoins me. We end up hanging out until the bar closes at 2 AM. Jay drives us back to the hotel. We're both completely exhausted, so we get ready for bed and don't stir until the following morning.

CHAPTER 10

Ace

* * *

I wake up a little before nine. I roll over and start rubbing Riley's hot little ass. She stirs awake as I run my hand along her side. She moans softly and turns to face me. She kisses me with more of an eagerness than ever before. As her tongue explores my mouth, I feel her hand slip inside my underwear. Her soft skin feels so good stroking my dick. All I can think about is plunging my dick as deep inside her as I can. I tug at her pajama bottoms. She lifts her ass and I pull them off, followed by her shirt. She frees my erection then kicks the covers off.

My eyes travel her body from head to toe. I will never get tired of looking at her, lying there completely naked. She reaches up and pulls me so I'm hovering over her. I feel her legs open. She grabs my hand and guides it to her pussy. I love a woman who knows what she wants and isn't afraid to take it. She's soaking wet and my fingers slide into her with ease. She grabs the extra pillows from the floor and slides them under her ass.

"Fuck me deep." she says in a husky voice.

I position myself completely on top of her, and thrust my dick inside her. The angle of her beautiful body lets me slide all the way in. I fuck her hard as my balls slap her sexy ass. I love everything about sex with this woman. The taste, the sound, the feel, even the way she smells when she's ready for me. Everything is perfection. Listening to her moans as my dick hits her g-spot is the hottest song ever written.

"Oh fuck, Angus, that feels so good." she moans.

I pull the pillows out and lay her flat. I lower myself and kiss her deeply while I slide in and out of her sweet body. There's something different between us this time. Love. Could she be falling for me the way I have for her? I'm still too afraid to say anything, so I keep my lips on hers as our tongues intertwine. I feel her quake as she screams out in pleasure. I feel her release soak my cock as I fill her with my seed.

"Mmm, that was incredible." I whisper as I hold her in my arms.

She sighs and lays her head on my chest. I feel my resistance slipping away. Before I slip and tell her how I really feel, I pull away and get out of bed. I can see the hurt in her eyes, but she doesn't say anything. I spend my entire shower berating myself, but I just can't take the chance of ruining the time we have left. After I'm done, she takes her shower.

I order room service while she's finishing up. We eat breakfast in silence, then get ready to return home. I take Riley to a couple more antique shops on the way home, and she seems to forget how I hurt her feelings earlier. I'm not particularly into this, but seeing the joy on her face as she walks around makes it all worth it. I would do pretty much anything to make this woman happy. If only I could do it for the rest of my life. I think about how this is already our eighth day together and I get sad. I don't want this to end.

"Oh my god, Ace, come look at this!" I hear Riley call from down the aisle.

I walk down and she's holding a record. She hands it to me and I'm looking at myself twenty years younger. I can't believe she found my band's debut album. I'd almost forgotten how long I used to wear my hair. I definitely couldn't pull off that look anymore. I hand the record back to her, but she doesn't return it to the bin.

"You're not buying that, are you?"

"Damn right I am. I love it!" she responds.

I smile at how excited she is that she found it. We walk around a little more before she heads to the front to pay for her find. After she's done, we drive a little while longer then stop for a quick bite at an outdoor cafe. After we're done eating, I get back on the road, stopping at the same overlook I took her too a few days back. I grab a blanket from the trunk, take Riley's hand and walk her to the same spot. After I spread out the blanket, we lay down together and gaze up at the sky.

I pull her into my arms and crush my lips to hers. We quickly tear each other's clothes off. There's something so primal about fucking in public. I'm not sure if it's the risk of getting caught or what, but I can't feel her skin on mine fast enough.

"Babe, outside is my favorite place to fuck you."

I don't wait for her response. Instead, my mouth covers hers as I get on top of her. She moans into my mouth as my dick enters her wet pussy. Each thrust feels better than the one before. No woman has ever felt this amazing. I truly believe we were put on this earth to be together. Her hands grab my ass and pull me in closer. Every inch of our bodies is pressed together as the world around us disappears. All there is in this moment is me and her. We quickly climax together. I wrap us in the blanket while we come down off of our sexual high. We get dressed before anyone sees us then lay in each other's arms until the sun goes down.

When we finally arrive back at my house, we head up to my bedroom. Within seconds, we're naked and in bed. I just can't get enough of this woman. We fuck for hours until neither of us has anything left to give. She's in my arms, head buried in my chest, and I want to keep her just like this forever.

"I can't believe we only have two days left. I'll have to come up with something epic to finish our staycation."

I'm suddenly overwhelmed by sadness that it will soon be time for this woman to leave my home. But not just my home. She'll be leaving my arms, and that's a level of pain I wasn't prepared for.

CHAPTER 11

Riley

* * *

I wake up and feel an overwhelming sadness. I can't believe it's already my ninth day with Ace. Leaving him after tomorrow is going to be one of the hardest things I've ever had to do. I feel tears forming in my eyes, and quickly wipe them away before Ace wakes up. He stirs a few minutes later and pulls me into his arms.

"Good Morning Baby." he says with a sleepy smile on his gorgeous face.

Forcing a smile, I reply, "Good Morning, Ace."

"Baby, you seem a little down this morning."

"No, I'm fine."

"You don't seem fine. Maybe some of my special brand of lovin' will help."

Before I get a chance to answer, he kisses me hard. I feel that familiar warmth sweep over my body just as it had every time I was in his sexy arms. He quickly gets me out of my pajamas, then slips his boxers off. I'm still impressed by his size and even more so, what he does with it.

"Baby, I never get tired of being naked with you."

"Oh Ace, you always make me feel so good."

He smiles at me, and my insides melt. He moves on top of me and slides inside me, taking my breath away, I moan as his dick moves inside me. There was more of a tenderness from him this time, as if he was making love to me instead of just fucking me. Or, maybe, it was my feelings of sadness that made it seem like something it wasn't. He came hard inside me, then used his magic fingers to send me over the edge. After holding me for a few minutes, Ace got out of bed and pulled his boxers on. I was about to get up when he stopped me.

"Baby lay back and relax. I'm going to serve you breakfast in bed today."

"That's really not necessary, I can come help you."

"No way, beautiful, this is your vacation and you deserve to be pampered. In fact, that's what today will be, a full day of me pampering you."

Ace returned a little while later with a tray of food. He made a delicious breakfast of eggs, bacon, and rye toast, all of my favorites. He also had coffee and apple juice for us. He put the tray on the night table and sat down in bed next to me then handed me a plate. After we ate, Ace put the empty plates back on the tray. He got up, walked over to the side of the bed and took my hand to help me up. Such a gentleman!

He led me into the bathroom and to the chair he had moved in there. Once I sat down, Ace poured some bubble bath into the tub and turned the water on. After the tub was full of water and bubbles, Ace helped me up. He walked me over to the tub and helped me get in, then climbed in next to me. He put some romantic music on then moved behind me. I leaned back against his chest and he massaged my shoulders. I felt so relaxed that I fell asleep in his arms. I woke up a while later and sighed with pleasure.

"Baby, we can stay in the tub as long as you want. Once you are ready to get out, I have some more things planned for you."

"As excited as I am to see what else you have in store for me, I want to relax a while longer." I reply.

"Sounds perfect, baby."

He keeps his arms around me as I rest against his sexy chest. I love everything about this man, but I still can't bring myself to tell him. Besides, after tomorrow, he can finally be rid of me and move on to the next one. Even as I think that, I'm not sure I believe it. It sure seems like he has feelings for me too, but who am I kidding? I'm way too plain and boring to be worthy of a hot rockstar like him.

Once I'm done soaking, I say, "I'm ready for what's next."

Ace gets out of the tub and wraps a towel around his waist. He then helps me out of the tub and wraps me in a towel, pulling me into his arms. He leads me over to the walk-in shower so we could rinse the bubbles off. We head back to his bedroom and once we're inside, he lays me down on the bed then removes my towel. He removes his own and joins me in bed.

"Baby, l wanna spend the afternoon in bed, pleasuring each other."

"Oh Ace, that sounds absolutely divine."

He flashes me those sexy dimples before he kisses me. The kiss was more tender and romantic but felt no less amazing. I open for him and our tongues intertwine as his hands caress my skin. Never breaking the kiss, he moves on top of me and gently enters me.

Just like earlier, his thrusting felt different this time, slower and more tender. I moan softly as he slides his arms under me, holding me close. I wrap my arms around him and began rubbing his muscular back and sexy ass. He groans as he continues his slow, rhythmic thrusting.

"Oh Ace, it feels so different this time."

"Is that good or bad?"

"Mmmm...it's sooooo good."

I lose track of how long we stay like this. Ace's slower pace is making it last, and delaying my orgasm. When he finally brings me to orgasm, I have the most powerful release I've ever felt. My body quivered as wave after wave of pleasure courses through my body. I scream in ecstasy as Ace continues moving inside me until I feel him explode. Our bodies are drenched in sweat from that incredible workout. Ace lies down next to me. I nestle into his arms and rest my head on his chest.

"Baby, would you like to go enjoy a picnic dinner? There's a campground not far from here."

"I'd love to. The forest is one of my favorite places...besides your bed of course!"

He smiles and kisses me gently. We get up, grab a hot, steamy shower together then head down to pack what we need. We carry everything out to the garage, load up the trunk of his Mustang and make the short drive to the Country Acres Campground in Gordonville, not too far from my favorite Pennsylvania town name, Bird-In-Hand. He takes us to one of the spots designated for tents. We get our tent setup then put our sleeping bags inside.

Ace builds a campfire and sets up the two chairs he brought. We sit down at the fire to enjoy the picnic he packed us. After we finish eating, Ace puts some music on. He stands and puts his hand out, so I take it. He pulls me into his arms as we sway to the music. We're completely lost in each other. He kisses me and I can tell from the eagerness that our tent is going to be rocking tonight!

When it starts to get dark, Ace safely puts out the fire and we clean up the area before we get into the tent. Ace opens up the two sleeping bags so we can lay together. He undresses me then himself and motions for me to lie down.

"Are you ready for more pampering, baby?"

"Oh Ace, you've pampered me enough already."

"There is no such thing as enough when you're on vacation. Now, lay back and let me work my magic."

I do as I'm told. Ace starts kissing my neck to start his journey. He takes each breast in his mouth, licking and sucking gently. I start moaning, thinking about where he will eventually land. He showers my stomach with soft kisses. He runs his tongue down until he reaches my pussy. He runs his tongue between my folds, stopping to tease my clit. I arch my back as my moaning gets louder. Nobody had ever made me feel as good as Ace does.

"Oh baby, your tongue feels so good. Please baby, go harder, don't stop baby."

Ace ignores my pleas and continues his slow and sensual pace. He's driving me wild as the pressure slowly begins. When I finally reach the boiling point, I experience an intense orgasm. Fuck, this man knows what he's doing. He doesn't stop and the pressure quickly builds on my already sensitive clit. He slides a couple of fingers inside me. It only takes a few strokes and my body explodes for a second time. This one was even more intense than the last and I scream. Ace slides back up so we're face to face.

"You taste so damn good, woman. What would you like now?"

"I need to feel you inside me. Please fuck me now."

"In due time. First, will you do something for me?" he asks me with a sly smile.

"That depends on what," I reply.

I watch Ace grab a book and flashlight out of his bag. He hands me the book and I blush when I see what it is. He hands me the latest book by talented local author Eden Davidson. I've seen her at our local rock club with Johnny, the sexy drummer she's married to. If her writing is any indication, Johnny is a very lucky man!

"Will you read a dirty scene to me?"

"Ummm..."

"What, babe? Don't tell me you're embarrassed after everything we did this week."

"Well, I guess not, but I'm a bit nervous."

"Trust me, you want to do this. I promise I'll make it worth your while."

I read him one of her naughtier passages and I giggle the entire time. I have no idea why I suddenly got so shy. When I finally finish the scene, I look at Ace and see that his dick is hard. Despite my laughing fit, I somehow managed to turn him on.

"Well, I did my part by reading to you. Now you damn well better do your part inside my part!"

Never one to disappoint, he moves on top of me. That intensity is back, indicative of how much hearing me read aroused him. We fuck like wild animals until the wee hours of the morning. After we're done and drenched in sweat, along with other fluids, we sneak to the campground's pool and take a secret skinny dip. When we're done, we wrap ourselves in towels and run back to our tent before anyone catches us. We cuddle up in our sleeping bags and hold each other close until much later in the morning.

CHAPTER 12

Ace

$$* * *$$

After we pack up the campground, we drive to one of the local diners and grab some breakfast. I can't believe we've already reached day ten. How the hell am I going to let this woman walk out the door? Once we've unpacked from the camping trip, we sit down on the couch. I turn to her, flash that smile that I've seen melt her, and cause her jaw to drop.

"I can't believe today's our last day together. Just you wait until you see what I have in store for you, doll!"

"Sounds like I'm in for quite a day." she says, a bit breathlessly.

"I know you remember when I took you on a tour of the house that there was one room I didn't show you."

"Yes, and honestly, I've wanted to ask, but wasn't sure I should."

"I wouldn't have told you. I was saving that for today. But first, let's shower."

As we ride the elevator upstairs, I think about how this is going to be a shower, and a day she'll never forget. We go into the bedroom and strip down. I watch as she reveals her sexy flesh and I lose control of my dick. I see her look down at my erection and lick her lips. Fuck, she's the sexiest woman I've ever known.

We get into the shower and I turn the water on, as hot as we can stand it. The hot water and the steam feel amazing. Now, it's time for me to make my woman feel just as amazing.

"Baby, go face the back wall and brace yourself." I say.

Once she's in position, I stand behind her.

"Spread those legs, woman."

I slide a couple fingers inside her, and fuck, she's already so damn wet. I fuck her with my fingers as she moans into the wall. Unable to wait one more second, I take my fingers out and replace them with my dick. I fuck her slowly, holding her tight so she doesn't slip. The hot water pounding my back while I pound her feels so fucking good that I quickly empty inside her. I slide my dick out of her sweet pussy, and finger her until she comes.

"Holy shit, Ace, that was so fuckin' incredible!" she says.

"That was only a preview of things to come, baby. Now, let's get cleaned up and on to our next adventure."

After our showers, we walk back to my bedroom.

"Take a seat on the bed, baby. And stay naked. I'll be back for you when I'm ready."

I walk down the hall to the secret room and grab the key from its hiding spot. I let myself inside and get everything ready. I just hope this won't be too much for her. I pull on my favorite black leather pants and black shirt. I leave half the buttons open to tempt her. I take a deep breath, and return to the bedroom. I keep my eyes locked on her pretty face as I approach the bedroom. Her mouth drops when she sees me.

"Oh my god, you look so damn sexy." she exclaims.

"Come with me." I command.

Like a good girl, she gets up and follows me down the hall. I hesitate for just a second before I unlock the door. Before I open it, I turn to her, and after eyeing her up and down, I put a hand on the doorknob.

"Baby, I want to spend the rest of our last day together in this room. I have to warn you, though, this will be unlike anything we've done so far. I'll need you to tell me if anything makes you uncomfortable."

"Ummm, okay, wow."

"I'm giving you one chance to change your mind. Otherwise, you'll need to be adventurous and willing to trust me."

"No way in hell I'm changing my mind. I want this."

"Then let's go inside and begin our journey."

* * *

* * *

Riley

* * *

* * *

I watch Ace's face light up when I agree to go in. He pulls me in tight and kisses me with more aggression than ever before. There's something in his kiss that lets me know I'm in for one hell of a ride inside this room. My heart starts racing and I'm not sure if it's from nerves, excitement, or a bit of both. I feel heat spreading the entire length of my body. Without a word he takes my hand and we walk inside. My eyes go wide when he opens the door and turns the light on.

The walls are painted red and there's a king-sized bed with a beautiful brass headboard in the middle of the room. The only other furniture in the room is a big, red chair, a small dresser and a refrigerator. I'm curious what might be in that fridge. Ace walks over to me and kisses me hard with that same aggression he had in the hallway. Without a word, he removes my clothing and lays me down on the bed. He puts on some sexy music and does a strip tease for me. Once he's naked, he walks over to the fridge.

"Close your eyes, baby, I have a surprise for you." he says in a sexy whisper.

After he returns to the bed and lays down next to me, he tells me to open my eyes. He's holding a can of whipped cream and a bottle of chocolate syrup.

"What are you planning to do with those?" I ask, though I have a feeling I know the answer.

Saying nothing, Ace opens the whipped cream and puts some on my stomach. He does the same with the chocolate syrup. My heart races with anticipation of what he's going to do next. Ace lowers his head and licks. Even after the whipped cream and syrup are gone, he keeps using his tongue on my belly before he moves lower. Damn, I love how his tongue feels on my pussy!

"Mmmm, Ace, so good baby."

He continues until I explode with yet another incredible orgasm. Still not saying a word, just smiling, he gets up and puts the whipped cream and syrup back in the fridge. He again tells me to close my eyes. I hear him open a drawer in the dresser then close it a couple minutes later. I hear him walk back to the bed. This time he stands next to the bed and tells me I can open my eyes. He has two silk scarves, a blindfold and a feather in his hand. My eyes open wide, but I say nothing.

"Baby, do you trust me?"

I nod yes.

"I need to hear you say it, doll."

"Yes, Ace."

I'm a little surprised, but I'm excited by what I think he has in mind for me.

"Good, baby. I'm going to put this blindfold on you then gently tie your wrists to the headboard. If any of this makes you nervous or uncomfortable, please tell me."

Feeling especially naughty, I reply, "Please baby, I want this too."

He flashes me the naughtiest, sexiest smile I've ever seen. I'm glad that's the last thing I see before he blindfolds me. I feel him take one of my wrists at a time and gently tie them to the headboard with the silk scarves. He puts the music back on so I can't hear where he is. The anticipation of when he'll touch me, where he'll touch me and how he'll touch me excites me like nothing ever has.

Suddenly, I can feel Ace's breath on my skin, so I know he's close to me. I feel the soft feather gently caressing my neck and continuing down my whole body. I'm on fire from head to toe. After he's done with the feather, he lets me lay there for a few minutes. I love not knowing what's coming next.

He lays down next to me and kisses me hard. I feel his tongue in my mouth. I intertwine my tongue with his as I return his kiss. I ache to touch him but I can't, which excites me even more. He continues down my body, showering me with kisses, but this time, he avoids the place I most want him to touch. I had no idea before today how much I would love this mild kink.

Unable to stand it any longer, I cry out, "Please Ace, touch my pussy. I'm throbbing for you."

He doesn't respond and he also doesn't touch, but I know he's close as again I can feel his breath on my skin. A little while later, I feel his fingers on my pussy, stroking my clit, and I moan loudly.

"Oh baby, you look so sexy tied to my bed. I need my dick inside you now."

"Ace, please baby, fuck me now. My pussy aches for your huge cock."

I feel him move on top of me and thrust his dick inside me hard. He pounds me hard and fast, groaning each time his dick moves inside me. I didn't think it would be possible for him to be any better than the other times we fucked, but holy shit, it was more incredible than anything I've felt so far. He explodes inside me then gets up and I hear the dresser drawer open.

I hear a buzzing sound and without warning, I feel strong vibrations on my clit. The toy is so powerful, it doesn't take me long to explode. Before I've even finished my orgasm, his dick is back inside me. Each time he fucks me and comes inside me, he uses the vibrator on me. Each orgasm comes faster and is more intense than the one before. We continue like this all afternoon and I lose count of how many orgasms we have. My throat's sore from screaming with pleasure all afternoon, but it was so fucking worth it.

"Damn, woman, you've completely worn me out," he says. "Close your eyes. I'm going to remove your blindfold."

When he's done, he unties my wrists. I slowly open my eyes to let them adjust to the light. I look at Ace and he has the biggest smile on his face. I can't stop smiling as my entire body tingles.

"I've never done anything like that before, Ace. It was the most incredible day yet."

"I had to make sure our last day together would be something you would NEVER forget."

"Oh, baby, you accomplished that."

Both sweaty and sticky from all the sex, not to mention the whipped cream and chocolate syrup, we shower together and get dressed. Ace prepares one last meal for us to enjoy together. Neither of us say much during dinner. After dinner, I help him cleanup then get my stuff together. Though I don't want to, it's time for me to head home and back to reality. Ace calls Bruce to take me home. He texts Ace when he arrives.

I'm about to open the door to leave when he grabs me and kisses me one last time.

"Thank you. I had an amazing time." I say as I fight back tears.

"It was my pleasure, baby."

Bruce drops me off and I go inside. As soon as I close the door behind me, the tears flow freely. I can't believe I'm never going to see him again.

Epilogue

RILEY

* * *

Monday arrives way too soon. Even though I spent them alone, these two weeks went fast. I've been dreading today, as I know everyone will be asking how my trip was. I can get away with generalities with most of my co-workers, but Maddie is going to want full details. That only leaves me one option. I have to tell her what happened. As if on cue, she appears at my desk, her usual cheerful self.

"Spill it, girl. How was your ten days in heaven?" she asks as she parks her ass on my desk.

I feel tears starting to prick my eyes. I look up at her and the smile disappears from her face. She grabs my arm and says, "Let's take a walk."

We go outside to the break area and sit down at an empty table. I fill her in about what happened and what I spent my time doing, including the story I wrote. She gives me a big hug.

"I'm going to find that fucker and cut his dick off." she shouts.

"No need. I'm over him. I never really loved him, anyway."

"No shit, I know who you love."

I fold my arms and say, "I do not."

"You keep telling yourself that. Now, you know I want to read that story."

"I figured you would. I have a copy in my bag."

We go back inside and stop at my desk so I can give Maddie the story. She takes it and skips away. She updates me each morning that she's still working her way through it and she'll let me know when she's done.

The rest of the week drags. When Friday finally arrives, I'm more than ready for the weekend. The weather is gorgeous out and I wish I was anywhere but here. I see Maddie approaching with a big smile on her face.

"Girl, that story was awesome," Maddie says. "Thank you for including me in it."

"You're welcome. If only parts of it could come true." I respond.

"I know. I still follow Ace on social media. Too bad he's not coming to our reunion."

"Me too, but I'm sure he's too busy for that."

"If he saw that fantasy you wrote about him, you can bet he'd be here."

"Yeah right. If only I was how I portrayed myself in that story. But, alas, I'm boring."

"Like hell, woman. Nobody who writes a story like that is boring. Can you imagine what it would feel like to get fucked by that man?" She smiles.

"I bet my story didn't even come close to how incredible he would be."

"Could you imagine if he got his hands on it?"

"I would die of embarrassment if that ever happened!"

"Or, maybe, he would want to start making some of that stuff come true. Especially the sexy stuff." she laughs.

I sigh as I enjoy the rest of my lunch break with my childhood best friend and now co-worker, Maddie Carson. I still remember how we met way back in the first grade. They always seated us alphabetically by last name, so I was right behind her. She turned around and just started talking to me on the first day, and we've been friends ever since. She is the keeper of my deepest secrets, especially the one that has me a mess right now.

I was actually glad to hear through the grapevine that a former classmate turned world-famous rockstar wouldn't be attending our high school reunion. I took a definite chance publishing that story. I made it clear in all disclaimers that it was completely fictitious, but Maddie knows otherwise. Sure, none of the stuff in that book actually happened, but I sure as hell want it to. Especially the naked parts.

Ace didn't join us until we were all in junior high. He just had it." All the girls went crazy when they saw him. For some reason, he chose to befriend Maddie and me. It may have had something to do with the fact that while all the other girls were following the latest pop bands, we came to school in hard rock band t-shirts, just like him. Our lunch break is winding down, so we gather our stuff and head back to our desks.

"Are you ready for tomorrow night?" Maddie asks.

"As much as I can be. I'm just glad I'll be there with you!" I reply.

"We're gonna have a good time. People are going to go crazy when they see the hotties we've become." Maddie says.

I laugh. "Thank you for always helping to build me up. I'd be lost without my bestie."

"You know I love you, girl."

"Love you more."

"I'll pick you up at 6:30 tomorrow!" Maddie says.

"Maybe you should come at 6, in case I need help. You know how bad I am at makeup and picking out outfits." I reply.

"I'm always here to help the beauty-challenged." she teases.

We've reached my desk, so I wave goodbye and she heads off to her work area. I yawn my way through the rest of the day. I'm grateful when 4 o'clock rolls around. I'm in serious need of some sun, so as soon as Maddie reaches my desk, we practically run out the door.

"What do you say to hitting the club tonight? They're having an outdoor night tonight." Maddie says.

"Sounds like fun. I could use a night out." I respond.

"Maybe we'll find hotties to hook up with. I really need some dick."

"Maddie!"

"Oh, don't pretend to be all innocent with me, girl. Remember, I read your story. I know whose dick you want!"

"Shut it, bitch!" I joke.

"How about you head over to my house around 5? I'll pick you out something to wear and get you ready." Maddie says.

"Trying to get me laid, or something?"

"Damn right, girl. We both need the cock!"

"That right there is why I love you, my friend!"

"Dirty girls, at your service!" Maddie jokes.

"Don't you dare use that line at the club!" I joke.

By the time we reach the parking lot, we're both laughing so hard, tears are streaming down our faces. We get in our cars and head home to get ready for tonight. I shower and throw on shorts and a t-shirt, since Maddie's going to give me something to wear. If I know her, she's going to have me showing more skin than I usually do. Fuck it, though, it's been way too long since I've gotten fucked and I'm horny as hell tonight.

I pull into Maddie's driveway a little before 5. She's waiting on her porch for me. She drags me right to her bedroom so she can show me the outfits she picked out.

"So, anything you like?" Maddie asks.

"I like the jeans and the black t-shirt." I reply.

"I had a feeling. Just to warn you, the t-shirt is low-cut."

"Maybe I should pick something else."

"No way, the guys will love it. Let's face it, your lady-balls are hot!" she says.

I laugh so hard, I can't respond. I get dressed then Maddie does my hair and makeup. She gets herself ready and we start the drive to the club.

It's still a little on the early side, so the crowd is just starting to gather. We're lucky and we get a decent parking space. We got to the patio area and found a table. A few minutes later, we have our food and drink order in. I see Maddie scanning the crowd, no doubt looking for some hotties! I start looking myself when I suddenly spot someone that makes my jaw drop. It couldn't be? I must be imagining him after writing that fantasy about him. I shake my head, trying to clear it when I see Maddie get up and approach

two guys. I can tell by her face and body language that she's flirting. Whatever she said to them worked, as the three of them walk to our table.

"Riley, I'd like you to meet Christian and Nathan. Boys, this is my
bestie, Riley."

Nathan, who's clearly into Maddie, nods while Christian sits down
next to me. He's cute enough but I find myself comparing him to Ace,
and nope, he just doesn't do it for me. But, since Maddie's so into
Nathan, I decide to be a polite wingwoman and talk to Christian.. He's
a nice enough guy, but that spark just isn't there. Meanwhile, Maddie
and Nathan are putting on quite the show on the dance floor.

I'm starting to get bored with Mr. Dull, so I look around and I see
someone looking my way. Holy fucking shit, it is him. I see him headed
my way, and every feeling in existence sends my stomach flipping. He's
exactly how I remember him, except a little bit older. Time has been
kind to him, and he looks even better than he did back in high school.
Maddie is so caught up with Nathan, she never notices.

"Hey, girl, there you are. I've been looking everywhere." he says with
a slight wink.

Taking his cue, I reply, "This nice guy was keeping me company
until you got here."

Christian's face drops, but he accepts his defeat, mumbles something unintelligible and races away from the table.

"You looked like you needed saving." Ace says.

"What the fuck are you doing here? Sorry for being so blunt, but
I'm in shock." I say.

"I came back for the reunion." he says matter-of-factly.

"What? I heard you weren't coming."

"That's what I wanted you to think. I wanted to surprise you. I
wasn't counting on seeing you here."

"Well you sure as shit surprised me. I thought I was seeing things
after writing, never mind."

"No way, you can't start that and not finish. What did you write?"

"Please, forget I said that." I beg.

"Can't. Tell me!"

"I kinda write steamy stories." I say as my cheeks catch fire.

"Is that so? I always knew there was a dirty girl in there somewhere. Dare I ask who you wrote about?"

"I'd really rather you didn't."

"Fine. Have it your way. For now, at least."

He doesn't give me a chance to respond. Without another word, he gets up and disappears into the crowd. I sit there with my mouth hanging open. I'm not entirely sure that just happened, but I know it did. I can't believe Maddie missed the whole thing. I desperately need to talk to her, but I don't have the heart to pull her away from Nathan, especially since his hands are kneading her ass like it's dough.

I can't sit here for one more minute, so I ask the bartender to call me a cab. While I'm waiting, I send a text to Maddie's phone so she doesn't worry. I imagine I'll get one hell of a story at the reunion tomorrow. Wait until she sees who's coming! I just wish I could have read more on his face. I have no clue if he was happy to see me, how he felt about me writing about him, or anything else. I get ready for bed, but sleep is nowhere to be found. I can't turn my brain off and I lay there staring at the ceiling for hours.

I'm up around 8 on Saturday morning, I finish up my cleaning and laundry then sit down to read for a bit. Around noon, my cell rings and I see Maddie's face on the screen.

"Hey, girl." I say when I answer.

"What the hell happened last night?" Maddie asks.

"You wouldn't believe me if I told you."

"Christian told Nathan and me that some guy came to the table."

"Not just some guy. It was Ace."

"WHAT. THE. FUCK?"

"I swear."

"What's he doing here?"

"He came for the reunion. He had told his friends to spread that he wouldn't be here as he wanted to surprise me."

"I don't understand."

"I'm not sure I do either. Tonight should be, um, interesting."

"No shit, captain obvious." She laughs.

"Enough about Ace. Tell me what happened with Nathan."

"Well, I just got home from his house. And damn did I have one hell of a night. He's an amazing fuck!"

"You gonna see him again?"

"We'll see. He said he would call me, but how often do dudes actually do that?"

"Hey, he could surprise you." I say.

"Not likely," she laughs. "Now, let's get back to Ace."

"I'd rather not. All that will do is freak me out for later. I need to find something to take my mind off of him until it's time to go tonight."

"Okay, are you dressed?"

"Of course. Why?"

"I'm on my way," Maddie says, then disconnects before I can protest.

I try to protest when she gets here, but she drags me shopping for something to wear tonight.

"Girl, you need to make Ace unable to resist you." Maddie said when she got here.

So, here I am, doing something I hate. I would much rather shop for office supplies or power tools than clothes and shoes any day. But I suffer through and by the time we're done, I do admit I'm going to look damn good tonight. When we're done, Maddie drops me off so I can shower and she lets me know she'll be over early to do my hair and makeup.

We get to the banquet hall where the reunion is being held. After we check in and get our ridiculous name tags, we head inside. I quickly scan the room, but there's no sign of Ace. Heads turn when we walk in. When our former classmates, most of whom picked on from K-12, realize it's me, their jaws drop. Good. I hope they're all sorry they never got with this. Assholes.

Maddie and I find an empty table and sit down. I keep an eye on the door, but still no Ace. I guess he's not coming after all. Oh well, even if he did, it's not like I would ever have a chance with him. Once the buffet is open, Maddie and I grab dinner and return to our table. After dinner, a DJ encourages everyone to hit the dance floor. After about five songs, he grabs a microphone.

"Riley Cavanaugh, please come to the dance floor." the DJ says.

I don't move, confused about why I'm being called up. Maddie finally grabs my hand and pulls me up. She drags me up front where I see a chair set up. The DJ points at the chair, so I sit down. Maddie stays nearby to make sure I don't take off. The DJ returns to his booth. I hear Def Leppard's Hysteria start and tears fill my eyes. This was Ace's and my favorite song when we were in high school. I lower my head and stare at my lap, hoping nobody will see my tears.

Suddenly, I feel a hand on mine and I look up and see Ace. He takes my hand and pulls me up. He walks me to the middle of the dance floor and pulls me in tight. Our bodies start swaying to the music when I feel his breath near my ear.

"Riley, baby, it's always been you," Ace whispers in my ear. "I'm in love with you."

I whisper back, "I'm so in love with you, Ace."

"You just made me the happiest man in the world. Now, let's get out of here and start acting out your fantasies."

Without warning, Ace scoops me up in his arms and carries me out. Goodbye, boring, predictable Riley Cavanaugh!

THE END

About the Author

Samantha Michaels was born in 1973 in the small town of Abington, PA and was raised and still lives in Hatboro, PA (both suburbs of Philadelphia). She is married to her high school sweetheart and they have a rescue dog, a beautiful Black Lab named Holly.

When she's not writing or working at her full-time job, she enjoys watching her Philly sports team (hopefully) win, listening to heavy metal/hard rock music, Texas Hold Em, reading, and spending time with friends and family.

Her love of reading began at a young age, thanks to her mother and Sesame Street. Her mom read to her constantly, and by three years old, she was reading on her own, and hasn't stopped. This eventually turned into a love of writing. She was writing for herself and then for a small group of friends, one of whom told her she should be writing books. She took her friends advice and has since published several romance books with plenty more on the way.

Also by
Samantha Michaels

www.ingramcontent.com/pod-product-compliance
Lightning Source LLC
Chambersburg PA
CBHW030539180626
46810CB00005B/1933